JUDGE LU'S CASE FILES

Stories of Crime & Mystery in Imperial China

P.A. DE VOE

Drum
Tower
Press

Printed in the United States of America

Publisher's Note: This is a work of fiction. Names, characters, places, and incidents either are the product of the author's imagination or are used fictitiously, and any resemblance to actual persons, living or dead, business establishments, events, or locales is entirely coincidental.

Cover design by P.A. De Voe

Published by Drum Tower Press, LLC

165 Bon Chateau Drive

Saint Louis, Missouri 63131-6081

http://padevoe.com/

LCCN 2019915365

ISBN 978-1-942667-16-2 (Paperback)

ISBN 978-1-942667-18-6 (Hardback)

ISBN 978-1-942667-17-9 (E-book)

To discover more stories about Imperial China, visit padevoe.com

CONTENTS

PREFACE

Robert van Gulik first brought the traditional Chinese detective story to Western audiences when he translated the only two Judge Dee volumes to which he had access. The books became quite popular and readers wanted more such tales. Without access to more stories, however, van Gulik decided to write them himself, all in the style of these long-standing detective stories.

I'd first encountered these tales years ago and was captivated by the crime stories—in particular their characters and how these lively tales revealed the everyday and legal culture of Imperial China. Through dynamic and engaging mysteries, we were able to peer into another world. A world which was both alien and familiar at the same time.

The original traditional detective stories van Gulik translated were written by an anonymous Chinese author and set in the Tang Dynasty. They were based on a real county magistrate and statesman, Judge Di Ren-jie, with the stories centering around his criminal cases. Besides Judge Dee (a variant spelling of Judge Di), there were many other well-known traditional magistrate tales, such as those of Judge Bao, a Song Dynasty official.

The early Chinese detective novels—composed with the intent of providing light, relaxing entertainment when groups of friends got together—included a heavy dose of the supernatural: ghosts, demons, and other paranormal experiences frequented the plot line. The authors and their listeners/readers believed the membrane between the natural and supernatural world was permeable and easily crossed over, thereby adding another possible dimension to their stories' development. All in all, van Gulik suggests that the long line of Chinese detective novels, going back well over a thousand years, was devised to entertain as well as reassure the audience that justice would prevail—whether in this life or the next.

While the short stories in this collection are modeled after traditional Chinese detective novels, they are written with the contemporary reader in mind. After all, the original magistrate tales are set relatively close to the cultural periods in which they were written. Close enough for audiences to share an intimate understanding of the setting's law, manners, and customs. For example, religious sensibilities and the basics of their legal system remained constant for hundreds of years.

Today's reader is, of course, far less immersed in medieval or imperial Chinese life. Therefore, the short stories in this mystery collection integrate contextual information about the early Ming Dynasty in order to bring that world to life for the reader.

———

Why is there an owl on the cover?

In traditional China, owls were considered a bad omen.

Although the bird represented mystery and secrets, owls appear on burial ceramics as far back as the Han Dynasty and were thought to forecast a death in the family. Such a harbinger of evil made the owl seem like the perfect symbol for Judge Lu's dangerous quest for justice and his battle against crime.

CHAPTER 1
JUDGE LU'S DILEMMA

A *magistrate's first duty is to the Ming Emperor through serving*
the people in his district.
He controls criminals and their destructive impact on the
community.
He brings a sense of fairness and justice, which prevents unrest
and revolt.
This is a simple task if the criminal behavior is from the lowly.
Not so simple if the illegal activities benefit the local gentry.
Every magistrate's success in office depends on the gentry's support.

The damp, sweltering heat was unusual for the fall, but neither man complained. The rain brought an end to the years of drought and famine that had plagued the region.

Wu Ming-feng smoothed his long gray robe, a sign of his elite status, and wiped his forehead with a green silk handkerchief. "Tomorrow's celebration will return our town to its former glory." Smiling, he added, "Pu-an is overflowing with people who've come for the banquet and commemoration. You've done our poor town a great service, Magistrate Lu."

"Not at all," Judge Lu returned. Wu's comment about him was a polite social convention. They both knew there'd be no celebration without Wu's financial backing. However, as owner of the largest silk company, the influx of outsiders into the town meant extra cash flowing into Wu's pockets. His support wasn't entirely altruistic.

"It's time to reinstate the annual celebration," Lu said. "The famines over the past ten years forced my predecessors to neglect this ceremony. Now, with your support, we can once more honor a filial son who exemplifies our country's most important value." Raising his cup, Lu continued, "Let's drink to Guei-qing, your youngest son, who will be honored in tomorrow's ceremony."

"Yes, while his brothers left to seek fame and fortune, Guei-qing remained at home."

As the men jointly raised their cups, the sharp sound of the petitioner's drum came from the court's front pavilion.

Someone was bringing a complaint before the court. Lu frowned. This was the first time since he took office a month ago that the drum sounded. This could be his first case. Still, he wondered at the late hour. What couldn't wait until morning?

A younger, more handsome version of the Judge stepped into the room. One glance at his brother and trusted secretary, Fu-hao, told Lu the problem was serious. He immediately rose. "I must attend to court duties, but I'll return as soon as possible." With that, he hurried from the room, his brother following.

"Who's the petitioner?" he asked.

"Widow Guo."

"Who is this Widow Guo?"

"She works land owned by her husband's clan since she has nothing of her own. She claims someone raped her daughter tonight."

"What happened? Who found the girl?" Lu's questions came horse-galloping fast.

"A farmer Song came along just as someone attacked Hua-er. The assailant fled. Song ran after him, but he got away. Song returned to the girl and took her home."

"Do they have any idea who did this?" Lu looked at Fu-hao as they strode through the hallways connecting his official residence to the court. He didn't miss his secretary's slight pause and nervous glance before answering. Lu prepared for bad news.

"Song said the rapist was Wu Guei-qing." Fu-hao spoke in a whisper as if to stay a pending disaster.

At that, Lu exhaled sharply. Wu Guei-qing? The one they were honoring as a filial son? How could this be? Lu closed his eyes. His first case. He saw his career slipping away before he'd even begun.

Entering the court chambers, Lu donned his official robe with its badge of office embroidered on the front and his stiff, black gauze hat. He took his place behind a massive, heavily carved desk. Fu-hao went to a side table where paper, ink, and brush waited for him to take down the petitioner's complaint. The court's constable and Lu's two personal retainers, Zhang and Ma, stood at attention along one wall.

"Bring in Widow Guo," Lu ordered.

As soon as the beleaguered mother was escorted in by the constable, she rushed forward and dropped to her knees. "Please give my daughter justice, Your Honor!" she wailed, tears streaming down her worn cheeks.

"Tell me all you know, leave nothing out," Lu encouraged her in a firm, gentle tone, even as he hated to hear what she had to say.

The elderly woman repeated much of what Fu-hao had told him. She named Wu's son as her daughter's attacker. At the end of her recital, Lu asked, "Where's your daughter now?"

"At home. She collapsed on her bed and hasn't moved since."

"All right. Tell me what evidence you have against Wu Guei-qing. Besides farmer Song's story."

"None, Your Honor, but Song is a good man. Why would he make such a thing up?" Her voice spoke volumes to Lu. She was conscious of the power and wealth of the Wu family. Plus, along with everyone else in the city, she must know Guei-qing's name had been sent to the Emperor and tomorrow he would be honored as a model of filial piety. Her charges against him would bring shame on him, his family, and the entire community.

"The court will investigate the matter. Return home. I'll come to talk to your daughter tonight. Do not discuss anything—anything—about the case with anyone." Lu's voice did not betray his anxiety.

When Lu returned to his office, his guest had already left. Lu's secretary and two retainers followed the judge, awaiting orders.

"What are you going to do?" Fu-hao asked. Because he was Lu's brother, as well as his secretary, he could ask the question no one else dared raise.

Lu knew what Fu-hao was really asking. Was he going to jeopardize everything by accusing the son of the most powerful man in the city of a crime on the word of an illiterate farmer and a distressed mother?

"What have any of you heard about Guei-qing? What's the word on the streets and in the wine shops?"

"He has a mixed reputation," Fu-hao conceded as he stroked his neck.

"He can be found every night at the local brothel and wine shop," Ma promptly added. "Gossip has it he spends his father's money faster than water flowing down a mountainside."

"So, he's out of control. Why hasn't his father forced him to behave? In the end, the father's responsible for everyone in the family," Judge Lu said.

They shook their heads. No answer.

Lu nodded. *One rash young man may destroy everything for me and my family.*

He removed his official robes and slipped on a long gray robe for traveling to the Guo's home. As magistrate, it was his duty to interview the alleged rape victim. He decided whether she was truly accosted or not. Then, as a matter of record, he sent a detailed report to his superiors. If anyone questioned the fairness of his actions, the report would be key to his superior's determination of malfeasance. Lu was keenly aware that he had a duty to fulfill, but he hoped the costs weren't too high.

"Fu-hao, we'll leave immediately. Bring your writing materials for the official report. Zhang and Ma, bring along a police officer and some torches."

When they entered Widow Guo's simple, earthen-walled home, his retainers' torches threw a pitiless light over the stark, bare room. Widow Guo's daughter lay in bed, a crushed butterfly struggling for survival.

Following the law's specific requirements, Lu gently slipped a hand under her chin and turned her face toward him. Ma's torch clearly illuminated the bruises around her mouth. As Lu began to describe his findings, Fu-hao took notes.

Lu pushed up the worn sleeves of her tunic. Raw, red bands encircled each wrist. Finally, he drew back her heavy cotton blanket. On her back—at her waist—were angry black and blue marks. A tear in her pants' waistband corresponded to the bruises on her back, as if the pants had been pulled sharply forward to rip them open. There were no bruises on the inside of her legs. Lu breathed a sigh of relief. *He must not have succeeded. At least she would not be condemned by society for her rape.*

Completing his examination, he pulled the blanket over her. "Hua-er, can you tell me who tried to rape you?"

The girl's eyes opened wide in terror, but she remained mute.

Lu sighed and laid a hand on her arm. "That's all right. Rest. Close your eyes. That's right." He moved away, signaling her mother to follow him.

"I won't need to speak further with your daughter. You may clean her up and get a doctor to care for her."

The mother, overwhelmed with grief, shook her head. "I've no money for a doctor. I'll tend to her myself."

"Don't worry about money. Get a doctor. Also, you must put your mark on the report of my examination verifying its accuracy." As with the majority of women, he realized she was uneducated. He handed her the writing brush and showed her how to make a mark.

She took the unfamiliar brush and, with hesitation, finally produced a black blob on the paper.

"Again, I must remind you to not talk to anyone. A loose tongue could destroy the court's investigation."

She nodded.

Lu immediately left for Song's house. He needed a statement from the farmer. Immediacy was critical, both to capture every possible detail of the event and—if Song was guilty of the crime—before he had a chance to solidify his story about the night's events.

Farmer Song's home didn't look much different from Widow Guo's, although the building and land was his. Ma pounded on the rough, planked door.

A disheveled young man opened it. He wore the typical farmer's work clothes of a short jacket tied with a thick cotton belt. It fell to his hips, covering the tops of his grass stained pants, which billowed out over his thighs to just below the knee.

"Tell me what happened," Lu said. His curt, no-nonsense approach aimed to intimidate, not terrify.

"I heard muffled cries..." Song began.

"Begin at the beginning. Why were you out at that time of night?"

Song nodded. "I have one pig and I want to breed her in another month."

Lu thought wryly he may be sorry he said "at the beginning," but let the young fellow continue.

"At times she escapes from her pen and goes to my neighbor's garden. He threatened to complain to our town's peace-and-security team. They could force me to pay a big fine for damages."

Lu glanced at Fu-hao, who was diligently taking notes, although a slight smile pulled at the corners of his mouth.

"I bought some really good, heavy wood from—"

"Get on with finding Widow Guo's daughter," Lu impatiently said.

Song nodded. "Anyway, I built a strong fence, but I still go out every night to make sure she hasn't gotten out. Tonight, she escaped again! Naturally, I headed to my neighbor's garden first. I took the path adjacent to the Guo farm and through the grove of trees just beyond it. That's when I heard these strange sounds and saw Hua-er on the ground. A cloth covered her mouth and another covered her eyes. A man struggled with her. I called out."

"Did you see his face?"

"No. When I yelled, he leaped to his feet and raced through the trees. I ran after him. I wanted to catch the rotten egg." A look of anger and disgust crossed his face. "He had too much of a head start on me. I had paused to check Hua-er, to see if she was okay. It was only a second, but enough time for him to get ahead of me.

"I didn't catch him, but I know who it was." He knit his eyebrows over dark, stormy eyes, and fell silent.

Impatiently Lu said, "Well, go on."

"Wu Guei-qing. The dog," he spat out.

Judge Lu's stomach tightened. "If you didn't see his face and he got away from you, how can you accuse him?"

Song stood with his feet apart and his arms crossed.

"Speak up," Lu roughly commanded. "You know the penalty for falsely accusing someone!"

"I didn't see his face, but I saw him. He was wearing a long gray robe; he was tall and overweight. Still, he ran at least as fast as me, so he had to be younger."

Lu appreciated the farmer's observation skills. Still, it didn't prove anything. It wasn't enough to bring a devastating charge against Wu's son.

"Take us to where you found them."

With Zhang and Ma lighting the way, they retraced his path to the grove of trees. Within a few feet off to the side of the path, Song gestured toward a trampled area. "There. That's where they were."

"What direction did the man run?"

"Through those trees, back to the path, and into the village. I lost him behind the Wu compound," Song added pointedly.

"Stay here while we inspect the grounds," Lu ordered. "Zhang, bring your torch and come with me. Fu-hao and Ma, inspect the other side."

Lu started with the area where the grass and small plants were crushed. A rope and a couple of green silk handkerchiefs lay in a pile. "Do you know about this?" he asked Song.

"That's the rope I cut off her wrists. Those two handkerchiefs were tied around her eyes and mouth."

Lu inspected the rope and its cut end, laid it down, and took up each of the pieces of silk. "Why is one cut and the other knotted?"

"The cloth covering her eyes was loose enough for me to push over her head, but I had to cut the one tied over her mouth."

Lu thoughtfully turned each over in his fingers as he inspected them. The silk was of the finest quality. He placed them in his sleeve and handed the rope to Zhang, who placed it in a satchel he carried for evidence. The two continued to inspect the ground and low-hanging branches, following a trail of broken tree limbs leading back to the path.

When they returned to the site, Fu-hao and Ma had finished their inspection.

"Anything?" Lu asked.

"The area to our south is trampled from the path all the way to this site. He must have grabbed the girl along the path and dragged her here. From the looks of it, she probably fought with him as he dragged her along because every few yards there is a wider spot which is trampled, indicating he had to stop to get a better hold of her."

Lu nodded. "All right. Song, show us where you ran after the assailant and where you lost him."

"This way," Song said and started off following the trail Lu had just inspected. Once they reached the walking path, he moved along the Wu family fields and their compound's massive walls. Arriving at a small servants' entrance door in the compound's wall, Song stopped.

"This is where he disappeared," he said.

"You saw him run right up to this spot?" Lu asked, steadily watching the young farmer.

Song's lips tightened. With a frustrated toss of his head, he said, "I didn't actually see him enter the Wu compound." He crossed his arms. "But I know he went in there. It was Guei-qing."

"You are accusing a man you never clearly saw and claiming he went into a house you never saw him enter," Lu shouted.

Song sneered. "You don't want to believe me because the Wu's are powerful and Widow Guo is poor."

Zhang swung at Song's head, hitting him with a powerful blow. Song lost his balance and fell; he lay splayed on the ground. "Show more respect!" Zhang bellowed.

Lu raised a hand to keep Zhang from kicking the farmer. Lu had to determine if this obstreperous young man was telling the truth or falsely accusing an innocent person. He turned toward the sergeant, who had followed behind them, and said, "Take Song to the jail."

Fu-hao sidled up to Lu and spoke softly to him. "There is no solid evidence to prove Wu Guei-qing did this thing. More than likely it was Song himself. He lives next to the Guo family and knows the girl and her habits. He could have attacked her from behind, blindfolded her so she wouldn't recognize him when he raped her, but then lost his nerve and pretended to be her savior. Such a crime is the act of an ignorant, immoral man—not of a gentleman," he added pointedly.

"The law cannot find a man guilty because he is poor and uneducated," Lu returned.

Fu-hao spoke more directly. "If you arrest Guei-qing, he will not be honored tomorrow as a model filial son. His family and the entire town will lose face before the world and —even more importantly—before the Emperor. In the end, through the power and influence of the Wu family, Guei-qing will be found innocent and you will be found guilty of malfea-sance. You will be thrown out of office, your career ruined. You will go to jail yourself, and our family will be ruined."

Lu looked steadily at his brother. What he said was true. Bringing a successful case against an influential gentry's son would be difficult under any circumstances. As presiding Judge, he would be held accountable for bringing a wrongful suit against such a man. What his brother also implied, and was true, was that Lu's entire family, including his brother, would suffer the consequences of such an error.

"What are you recommending?" Lu asked.

"Certainly, Song is the guilty party. He'll definitely confess under torture. He's a simple farmer who acted on impulse. He won't be able to resist telling the truth once the jailer gets a hold of him." His brother spoke with conviction. "The case will be over. No one will challenge Song's guilty verdict."

Lu stood in quiet thought, feet apart, hands tucked into his wide sleeves. Again, his brother was right; no one would question his decision if he found Song guilty. On the other hand, accusing Guei-qing would open up a world of trouble. The Wu family, the town, and even his superiors would challenge his decision. If he condemns Song, he will be praised; if he arrests Guei-qing, his decision opens the road for potential disaster.

He pulled the silk cloths out of his sleeve and stared at them for a long time. Finally, he stuffed them back into his sleeve and turned toward his men.

"Come, we have work to do," he said. He spun on his heels and strode away, around the compound walls. At the front gate, he nodded for Zhang to announce their presence.

Lu's guard pounded on Wu's massive wooden door, shout-ing, "Open up by order of the Magistrate!"

The entrance screeched open, revealing a befuddled servant.

"Take me to Wu Guei-qing immediately," Lu ordered.

The servant paused, as if not quite understanding what was happening. Zhang shouted, "This is Judge Lu, Magistrate of the District. Do what he says!"

The servant jumped to obey, leading them through the compound.

At Guei-qing's room, Zhang pushed the door open and held the torch up as Lu entered with Fu-hao. Sprawled on top of the bed, Guei-qing still wore his long gray, dirty, grass-stained outer robe. At their intrusion, Guei-qing lurched into a sitting position.

"What're you doing?" he asked, his voice slurred. He stumbled as he attempted to stand near his bed. The stench of wine filled the room. Staring groggily at the men in the doorway, he recognized Lu and drew back, shivering. "Why are you here? I haven't done anything!"

Zhang stepped forward. "Silence! The Judge will do the talking!"

Guei-qing staggered back.

"What is the meaning of this?" an irate voice demanded. Guei-qing's father stood in the doorway, his face contorted in anger.

"Wu Ming-feng you may remain in the room, but you must be silent while I interrogate your son," Lu said.

"Interrogate my son? What're you talking about?"

"If you are silent, you may remain. Otherwise, you will go outside," Judge Lu repeated, ignoring Wu's questions.

Guei-qing's father shot him a hostile look. "Do you know what you're doing? You'll regret this, Lu."

Zhang stepped toward him, but Lu stopped him. Without another word, Lu turned toward the quivering son.

"We know you accosted Guo Hua-er tonight. Confess, or you'll be arrested and the jailer will interrogate you."

Guei-qing's face lost all color. The jailer would certainly

use torture to get him to confess. He cast a pleading look at his father, but Zhang stepped closer to the elder Wu, reminding him to remain silent.

"No, no. I've been here, sleeping all night," Guei-qing stammered.

Lu scrutinized his clothing. "The criminal wore such a robe and knelt in the wet grass. How do you explain those stains?" Lu said, waving his hand toward Guei-qing's clothing. He then produced the silk handkerchiefs. "I believe these are yours."

Guei-qing looked down. "I didn't mean to. I was drunk. She was walking down the path, alone. It was an accident."

His father, shocked, started forward, but Zhang again blocked his way.

"An accident?" the judge roared. "You call rape an accident?"

"I was drunk," he whined.

Lu turned toward Fu-hao, who had already established himself at Guei-qing's desk. "Are you ready to write this down?"

Fu-hao hurriedly finished preparing his ink and took several sheets of paper out of his packet. "Yes, ready."

"Proceed," Lu instructed the young man.

"She shouldn't have been alone at that time of night." Sweat beaded on his forehead. His eyes sought his father and he said: "I was returning from a visit with friends," as if that explained everything.

"You mean you were returning from the wine shop," Lu said.

He grimaced and glanced down. "Yes. I said I was drunk," he whimpered.

"Go on," Lu ordered.

"It was too much. She swung a basket as she walked ahead of me. I thought, well, she doesn't even know I'm here. I grabbed her from behind and covered her eyes so she wouldn't recognize me. She started screaming, so I had to tie another handkerchief around her mouth. But she wouldn't stop struggling. She was hard to control. I found a long piece of rope in her basket. I grabbed it and tied her hands behind her back. She kept wriggling, trying to escape. Then that stupid farmer came along and almost caught me." He frowned and looked up. "She was so much trouble. If only she would have kept quiet, none of this would have happened."

Disgusted, Lu said, "Zhang, take him to the jail."

At that, Guei-qing shot another glance at his father, then spoke urgently. "Please, Your Honor, give me a few moments of privacy. I need to change clothes before leaving the house."

Lu paused, then ordered everyone from the room. "We'll be right outside. One of my officers is at your window. You can't escape."

Dejected, Guei-qing nodded.

No one spoke as they waited. After some time, Lu told one of his soldiers, "Go get the prisoner. He's had enough time."

The solider marched into the room but returned alone. "Sir, you need to come inside."

Lu and his men, with Guei-qing's father close behind, entered the room. The accused man lay bleeding on the floor. His father cried out and ran to his son's prostrate body.

He had cut his own throat, severing the windpipe.

Before the grief-stricken father could drop to his son's side, Zhang pulled him away. Lu strode forward. Guei-qing was dead.

Lu picked up a knife lying next to Guei-qing's hand. He had chosen suicide rather than jail and a trial.

Allowing Wu to care for his son's body, Lu and his staff left.

As he sat at his desk finishing the case file, Fu-hao said, "You took quite a chance."

Lu shook his head. "It's my duty to make sure justice is served for everyone, not just the powerful and wealthy."

Fu-hao sighed and nodded. "What about the girl?"

"I'll order Guei-qing's father to pay a fine covering the girl's medical expenses and to give her a dowry, which will allow her to marry well. But, now," he continued, "let's get a couple of hours sleep before court opens tomorrow morning."

Originally published as "Judge Lu's Dilemma, from the Judge Lu's Ming Dynasty Case Files" in *Fish or Cut Bait: A Guppy Anthology*, ed. Ramona DeFelice Long (Wildside, 2015), pp. 20-29.

CHAPTER 2
LEGACY

"A village elder just reported a suicide at the home of Master Tong Hong-gui." Fu-hao slicked his hair back and shook his head in disapproval. "We'd barely settled in when we had that terrible rape case and now we have a suicide!"

Judge Lu, who was sitting at his desk reviewing the local tax reports, perked up. He looked at his younger brother. When the judge took this position as magistrate in Jiangxi's Ji-an prefecture, his brother came with him as his official secretary.

"Who is this Master Tong, and what do we know of his family?"

"Tong Hong-gui's the head of the wealthy Tong clan, making him one of the most influential men in the area," Fu-hao said. "According to the elder, the woman was a young servant in the Tong household. She's from a mountain village and has worked for them less than a year. She often seemed moody and had a difficult time adjusting to being away from her home village. The elder also noted that Master Tong realized how busy you are with your many responsibilities, so he volunteered to take care of the disposal of the body, including an appeasement of her spirit." Fu-hao watched his brother and then quickly added, "As long as we have a report on her suicide, his offer could save you trouble and costs."

Without comment, Lu pushed back his chair and stood up, throwing off his official robe.

"Zhang, bring my riding cloak and tell Ma to bring along a couple more guards in case we need them. We're leaving immediately to inspect the body. Fu-hao, tell the elder to return to Master Tong's home. Tell him to leave everything in place; don't move the body or disturb the room she died in. We'll be there shortly."

Fu-hao sighed. "There is no merit in this case for you. Suicides are messy. Let the local powers-that-be take care of it."

Lu shook his head. "You know that, as judge, I should inspect the body and verify the suicide as such."

"The last judge didn't do that. He sent in reports as given by the local leaders. It was accepted by the higher courts."

"It was accepted, but it's not protocol. It's not correct." Lu took up the robe Zhang handed him and slipped it on. "Bring your writing materials for the report. We'll leave as soon as the horses are ready."

When the entourage reached the Tong home, Master Tong was at the gate to meet them. Judge Lu dismounted and came forward. As he approached, the robust, middle-aged man bowed, hands clasped together.

"Magistrate Lu, what an honor to meet you. I am sorry I have been remiss in coming to formally greet you earlier. This is an unfortunate affair for our first meeting." He swept his hand toward the door. "She killed herself in the storage room.

We were just beginning to take care of the corpse when we received word to stop. Let me show you the—"

"That will not be necessary," Judge Lu interjected. "I want you and everyone in the household to remain outside."

Master Tong looked taken aback and was about to respond when Lu added, "Please do not take offense. This is simply the normal procedure. We will inspect the body and the area for the official report. We will take care of the body. All expenses incurred will be covered by the court. You and your family should not have to pay for this unfortunate event."

Appearing somewhat mollified, Master Tong shifted back and forth from one foot to the other. "Yes, yes, of course. As the new magistrate, you may have a different way of doing things." He smiled, but the smile did not reach his eyes.

Leaving a couple of his guards at the gate to keep the curious and potential trouble makers away, the judge and his men entered the house.

At the storage room, he posted Zhang at the door and Ma at the open window. The early morning light flooded the space, revealing sacks of grain and covered jars of various shapes and sizes. Several open beams marched cross the ceiling. Under them the body of a small woman lay on the ground covered by a sheet. Beside the body sat a roughly made wooden stool with a long sash draped over it.

Fu-hao set his table under the window and prepared to record the judge's findings.

Removing the sheet, Lu quickly inspected the corpse. There were no unusual markings on her body, although he noted her unusually round belly. Rather big for such a slender person. Next, he observed her neck. The marks on her neck revealed a definite braid-like pattern. There was another smooth line, but it was shallow and not as dark.

He moved onto her face. She had clearly been a stunning

beauty when alive. Her wide-open eyes and mouth seemed to call for help. He passed his hands over her eyes, closing them.

Her hair was disheveled in spite of a phoenix-shaped, cloisonné hairpin tucked into the top of her ink-black hair.

Turning her over, he again noted the braid-like pattern on the back of her neck. Seeing nothing else of significance, he covered the body and stood up, stretching his back.

"A clear case of suicide," his brother said wiping the extra ink off his brush. "These young women are so foolish. Too emotional."

The judge examined the overhead beam. It was a good eight feet off the ground. The wooden stool was about a foot high. "We'll take the stool with us," he said. "This wasn't a suicide. She was murdered and the murderer tried to make it look like suicide. The marks on her neck indicate she was strangled with a rope; later, the smooth sash was tied around her neck. Plus, she's quite small in stature and, even standing on the stool, she'd never be able to get that sash around the beam she was supposed to have hanged herself from. No, she was definitely killed. The questions are why and by whom?" He looked down at the young woman's body. "I suspect she was pregnant."

Fu-hao started. "Pregnant? How could you know that?"

"Her stomach area is quite round and firm indicating she was pretty far along," Lu said. He glanced up at his younger brother's apparent naiveté.

"There's a reason for suicide," his brother said, "and possibly for murder." He frowned. "What an unfortunate turn of events for the Tong family. There will be lots of rumors, no matter what is determined. You'll have to be really careful handling this case. If their reputation is besmirched, you can be sure, you—we—will feel the full ire of Master Tong, his immediate family, and his whole clan. We'll both be ruined, with no future positions in sight!"

Judge Lu frowned deeply. "Don't dramatize the situation."

"I'm not. You know perfectly well how these things work. You are an outsider here, and new in your post as magistrate, no less. You don't have allies at the local or national levels. The Tong family is an important and wealthy clan. If it comes down to a battle between you two, no matter what the original 'facts' of the case are, guess who'll win." He struck the table. "Father put everything into you and your education. You will have failed our family before you've even began your career."

"Failed? How could I have failed the family?" Judge Lu's voice was low and tense. This was no time to argue, but his brother's implication struck him to his very center. He took a deep breath. "Write everything I've noted here in your notes and put it in the report. Now, I need to talk to Tong family members and their servants. You will record our conversations."

Clearly irritated, but saying no more, Fu-hao prepared a new set of blank sheets and began rubbing the rectangular inkstick over his simple gray inkstone until the liquid in its depression was a rich, vibrant black.

"Zhang!" His guard immediately stepped inside the room. "Bring in every Tong family member, beginning with Master Tong. After that, I want to talk to each of the staff. Tell everyone not to discuss this case with each other. Anyone who discusses it with another will be put in jail and beaten for contempt of court."

The judge and his staff spent the rest of the morning and half the afternoon interviewing every person who lived in the house or who might have had contact with the young maid. They worked through lunch, not even stopping for tea. By mid-day, when they finally finished, they were exhausted.

According to the servants, it was no secret that the Master had begun abusing her from when she first arrived at the house as a maid eight months ago. The other maids who shared her quarters had all noticed she no longer had periods and they believed she was pregnant.

Later, back at the office, Judge Lu went over the findings with Fu-hao, Zhang, and Ma. They all realized the evidence strongly suggested Master Tong was the father of the young maid's baby, but did that mean he would have killed her or have her killed?

"Such a powerful man can't be accused of murder on circumstantial evidence," his brother said.

"I know," Lu replied testily. "But such a man can't go free, either. Justice must be done."

Fu-hao shrugged. "It's time to be realistic. If you don't have better evidence, accusing Master Tong will be the death sentence of your career, not to mention the ruination of our family."

Judge Lu bit back a reply to his impetuous younger brother. Many friends of his father's, all having served for a time as magistrates or in other governmental positions in the national bureaucracy, knew the importance of having a trusted assistant when taking on a new post in a strange part of the country. They all strongly encouraged him to make his brother his personal secretary. Who else besides a close relative could he trust with such a position? His secretary would know the most intimate details of his work. His success would be completely aligned with his secretary's success in a way not possible with anyone else. In such a context, Fu-hao was the only logical choice for the position. But his little brother could be unpredictable. Like now, when he argued in this fashion, in front of Lu's official staff, Lu regretted his decision. He glanced at his sibling and then over at his guards. Somehow, Fu-hao had never learned when to engage in a brotherly argument and when to hold back. Any other secretary would simply follow orders.

Lu sighed and took up his brush as if to work on a report. "You may all go to supper. I'll call you together later." He did not wait for a reply before bending his head over his papers.

Once alone, he gently ran his fingers over the inkstone his father had given him when he passed his first set of national exams. A failure? Would his father consider him a failure if he pursued this case as a murder instead of calling it a suicide?

He quickly strode into the adjacent hall leading to his private quarter and the temporary altar he'd set up in honor of his ancestors during his tenure as magistrate in Ji-an. He placed three incense sticks in a carved copper vase in front of his father's image. Stepping back, he kowtowed three times and remained supine on the floor in front of his father's tablet.

Troubled, and in need of guidance, he naturally came to his father, dead these many years but always with him. He let the thoughts about the case run through his mind without editing, without trying to assert one side or another. Simply letting his father know. Hoping for direction.

His brother was right; his decision would impact their whole family, even the most extended—cousins and uncles. He needed to be mindful of the whole, of all the people who could be impacted: his family, his extended family, the Tong family and the Tong clan. But what about justice for the young woman, the most vulnerable and without family to fight for her? Did she truly commit suicide, considered the most reprehensible act because it insults the person's family and all their ancestors? And if it was murder, which he believed it was, should the murderer go free?

He laid on the hard-stone floor until exhaustion overtook him.

In the shadowed corner of the room he noticed a vague figure move forward. His father. Lu started to rise to kowtow again. His father raised a hand, stopping him.

"Remember what's important: 'Toward the humble, no arrogance; toward the strong, no compromise,'" he said. Pointing a finger at the pile of papers Fu-hao had laid on Lu's desk to review from the day's activities, he quoted the Analytics, saying, "'The objective of the superior man is truth.'"

With that, he turned and faded into the shadows.

Lu laid on the cold stone floor, head down, eyes closed for some time. His father had spoken. Lu knew what to do.

He returned to his office and prepared a formal invitation for this evening's dinner, then had it delivered to Master Tong. He ordered tea and called in Fu-hao, Zhang, and Ma. They found him relaxing at a low table. Since they had already started forming a tightly knit band around Lu, they automatically joined him when he swept his hand forward indicating they should sit.

After a short rehashing of the evidence, Judge Lu leaned back. "Master Tong will share dinner with me tonight," he said. At their surprised glances, he went on, "I am going to discuss the details of the murder with him and I want you, Fu-hao, to remain behind the screen at the end of the room and take notes on the conversation and what happens. Zhang and Ma, I want you two to guard each door. He will be here shortly."

Without comment, not even a word from Fu-hao, they left to take up positions. When Judge Lu entered the banquet room, which was already prepared for his dinner guest, his servant announced Master Tong's arrival.

Entering, Master Tong bowed low and, after exchanging courtesies, took a seat at the table. They ate and drank without mentioning the unfortunate day's affair. Instead, the judge centered on topics of local interest: how the crops were doing compared to the past three years; how many young men were preparing for the national examinations and who had passed the examinations last year; how many travelers passed through the area and the impact they had on the local economy. General, non-threatening topics. All the while, Lu encouraged his guest to drink more wine while pretending to match him cup for cup.

Finally, the judge came around to the young woman's death.

"Murdered. The thought is awful, isn't it?" Master Tong said, eyes on his half empty wine cup. He looked up at the judge. "Do you have any idea why such a thing would happen?"

"I'll tell you, but don't tell anyone else." The judge paused.

Master Tong shook his head, "Never."

"She was pregnant."

Master Tong went white. "No. How did you find out? Will my household be held responsible?"

"As her master, her behavior certainly reflects on you. But, she was a young country girl..."

"Yes," Master Tong anxiously interjected. "And, you know how those girls are: loose morals. Vixens. Ready to entrap any healthy man in their reach."

The judge took up his cup and pressed it to his lips. "Hmm."

Apparently taking Lu's murmur as a sign of agreement, Tong went on about the many servant girls he had heard about who brought ruin to the families they worked for.

"They could be taken in as the lover's concubines," Lu suggested thoughtfully.

"Bah. Then they'd become a burden to the household. They'd do little to no work, and if the child lives, they'd demand a share of the inheritance. It could be a nightmare for the man and his family." He threw back another cup of wine. "Besides, even a concubine needs to have some measure of sophistication."

"She was quite a beauty," Lu offered.

Tong sneered. "A rare beauty, it's true. But what of it? I am old enough to know how quickly enchanting, youthful beauty is lost. Especially after a child is born and the woman's place is secured."

"So, you think she was..."

"Another gold-digger. Looking for a man to keep her so she could lay around and not work. Probably using the fact she was pregnant as a one-way ticket to nirvana." He laughed. "It turned out to really be a one-way ticket to nirvana."

"The thing is," Judge Lu said, his eyes on Tong and his voice neutral, "rumor in the household has it that there was only one person she was involved with." He reached out and filled Tong's cup again.

Tong paused, looking at Lu. Then he reached out for his cup and downed half the liquid. "We're men of the world, Lu. I know what you want. Your esteemed predecessor had similar needs. This office is expensive; you have costly responsibilities. I can help you."

"And in return?"

"A report on the death being a suicide, of course." He finished his wine. "It's not that difficult and, as you know, such women can cause no end of trouble. They must be exterminated."

"Exterminated? Isn't that harsh?"

He slammed the cup down on the table. "No! These women... They entice, entangle their besotted prey, using their beauty and charms, but it's all a game to steal and control. They're a clear danger."

"Is that why she had to be stopped?" Judge Lu asked

softly, filling Tong's cup once again. "Why you had to kill her?"

"Yes. I knew you'd understand," Tong said with a nod.

"And the suicide?"

Tong laughed. "Getting rid of a body isn't always easy. Faking a suicide is. Especially for someone like her because she was given to moodiness. And who would question it?" Bleary eyed, he glanced over at Lu. "Except you. You're darn careful and observant. You'll make a lot of money as a magistrate, that I can tell you." He finished off the newly filled wine cup and shakily stood up. "Don't you worry about my appreciation for your help in this case. I'll have my servant bring a welcome gift to you tomorrow."

Judge Lu stood at the same time. "You won't have to bother with the welcome gift, Master Tong." He turned toward the screen and told Fu-hao to come out.

As Fu-hao appeared with his papers and brush, Tong staggered backward and fell into a half-sitting position.

"I'm lost," he said, dropping his head and covering his eyes with his hands.

"Zhang! Ma! Come and escort Master Tong to the jail cell. He'll be staying with us."

Originally published as "Legacy, from Judge Lu's Ming Dynasty Case Files" in the online magazine *Kings River Life* (2014): http://kingsriverlife.com/06/14/legacy-a-fathers-day-mystery-short-story/

CHAPTER 3
RECKONING

T he early morning drizzle soaked Judge Lu with unease as he leaned over his horse. He carefully directed his steed over the muddy path, negotiating the many holes carelessly filled in with rocks. He'd have to talk to the city headman about properly repairing the road. His companions, two personal guards and his brother Fu-hao, who also served as his court secretary, were being just as watchful in guiding their steeds. All of which made their travels slow-going.

Lu could have taken the official covered carriage to make his first courtesy call on Magistrate Yu Jiao in Nanchang, the neighboring prefecture, but he much preferred riding, whatever the weather.

Fifteen years Lu's senior, Yu Jiao had a wealth of experience and, most importantly, seemed willing to share it with Lu, himself a newly minted Magistrate. Lu knew what the law required of him as judge, investigator, prosecutor, and jury in criminal and civil litigation, and he had successfully resolved a couple of cases since his recent assignment to Pu-an. Nevertheless, he was painfully aware of his inexperience. His training as a Confucian scholar, required of all government officials, in no way prepared him for the practical job of running a prefecture. He gratefully spent hours with Yu Jiao discussing the responsibilities and pitfalls of their duties.

Rounding a thicket, a covey of three men and a wizened woman stood shrouded in the dreary, wet day and blocked the narrow pathway. One strongly built fellow addressed the others, while gesturing broadly toward an adjacent field with a hoe wielded in his left hand. The other men, burdened with sagging, enclosed baskets hanging at the ends of poles balanced on their shoulders, vigorously nodded as if in agreement, causing the baskets to swing precipitously. The woman stood apart, clutching a large bag to her chest.

The speaker spied Lu and his entourage and promptly stepped toward them. Lu noticed the infernal mud clinging to his shoes and leggings.

"Magistrate Lu," he said, bowing. "How auspicious for you to appear at this moment. I am He Qi-feng of Pu-an. My farm is southwest of here." He waved a hand in a general southwesterly direction. "I come along this path every day going to my field. Today I found farmer Chen laying at the end of the field and partially on the path. I am sorry to report he's dead. I have already sent another passerby to inform the city's headman."

"Is the headman here?" Judge Lu asked, surveying the group. No one stepped forward.

Qi-feng spit on the ground and said, "He's on his way." He looked down the path toward the town. "It may be a while; he often feels he's too busy to respond with immediacy."

Silently noting the unsolicited disapproval this comment carried, Lu dismounted, his shoes sinking into the road's muck. His two personal guards, Ma and Zhang, had already preceded him and were loudly ordering the small collection of bystanders to step aside. They parted, exposing a figure sprawled half in the field and half across the raised path.

Lu ordered Lu Fu-hao, his brother and the court secretary, to take the onlookers' names before they dispersed. As magistrate, Lu was required to examine the body and determine cause of death. In his opinion, if the man was murdered, valuable information could be exposed if there were witnesses to the process.

Once Fu-hao took their names, he returned to Lu's side. Normally, Fu-hao would record the examination as Lu carried it out, but with the persistent light shower this was impossible. He would simply witness the examination and record the event later after they returned to court.

Lu lost no time in doing what he considered to be the most onerous part of his duty as magistrate: a preliminary and thorough examination of the body. Crouching over the corpse and speaking quietly, to keep his voice from carrying, he noted his findings to Fu-hao. "The man is lying face down, right hand extended out onto the road, left hand down along his side. The handle of a small rice sickle protruded out from under the lower torso."

Lu inspected the back of the dead man's head. His soaked, matted hair formed a close-fitting hat. Ma turned the corpse over and Lu continued his examination and dictation. "The right side of the man's face is crushed." Lu looked at the pathway. "The man is lying face down in a rock-filled hole.

"A long, jagged cut is also apparent in the farmer's mud soaked, cotton jacket." Lu removed the rope belt, opening the jacket and revealing a deep slash stretching across his stomach. Gently pushing the dirt out of the wound, Lu measured the cut's length and depth. After giving the details to Fu-Hao, he said: "The wound's size and shape match a rice sickle's serrated edge."

Relieved to have that over with, Lu straightened and smacked his hands together to get rid of the dirt. Zhang brought him a towel to clean his hands.

"Looks like an accident," Fu-hao said.

Lu stared down at the body, then slowly nodded. "Yes. He could have slipped as he stepped onto the path. With this rain, the walls of the path are nothing more than mud. Then, since he was apparently carrying his sickle, it cut into his abdomen, killing him."

He remained silently contemplating the form on the ground.

"Something's bothering you?" Fu-hao said and sighed loudly. Lu knew the sigh was meant to be a complaint. Fu-hao often criticized him for being overly cautious, too slow to make a decision. Caution was not a problem his impatient brother had, Lu thought.

"Yes. I feel I am missing something important, but I just don't know what," he said, ignoring his brother's sigh. Lu shook his head and scowled.

"You're always looking for complications even when there aren't any," his brother murmured. Then, in a louder, official tone, said, "The report will say accidental death then?"

Lu stroked his ear. "Yes. There's no apparent reason to delay his burial."

Before he finished speaking, an older man hurried up to him, his long, gray coat flapping around his ankles. He halted before Lu and, hands clasped at the waist, bowed. Lu noticed the aged woman he had seen previously remained standing behind the other bystanders and at a slight distance. Her long, dank, unkempt hair made her appear more specter than villager.

With his eyes on the corpse, the stranger quickly introduced himself as the headman. "I heard you say this was an accident," he said. "What bad fate! What did he do to earn such bad karma?"

"To die at a young age is indeed unfortunate," Lu said.

The man sadly shook his head. "Farmer Chen was an only

son, newly married, with no offspring. He's the last of his family's branch."

"Ah," Fu-hao loudly sighed again, this time in sympathy with the deceased.

"Bad fate, indeed," Lu said and glanced from the village elder to the corpse. The last of his line meant there was no one to feed and care for his needs in the netherworld; he would become a hungry ghost, terrorizing the living.

"I understand He Qi-feng alerted you about farmer Chou's death," Lu said.

The headman cast a quick glance at Qi-feng, who had moved down the path. "Yes, yes. He sent someone else to come and report the tragedy to me. He didn't come himself. He never does."

To Lu, a clear note of unsolicited disapproval was embedded in the last comment. There seemed to be a bit of tension between Qi-feng and the elder. Regardless, their issue was surely unrelated to this incident and, therefore, none of the court's business.

Having determined the death was accidental, Lu released the body into the hands of the village headman and went back to the *yamen* where he would write up his findings and Fu-hao would complete an official death report.

On the way back, Lu reminded himself to be sure and make the necessary ceremonial offerings to those unfortunate enough to have died without descendants to care for them in the afterlife. As one of the duties of his office, it must be done properly in order to diminish the possibilities of hungry ghosts causing trouble among his province's citizens.

Three days later, as Lu poured over maps showing Pu-an's land ownership patterns, the beat of the petitioner's drum in the court's outermost courtyard caught his attention. Absently, he shuffled the papers together and began putting them aside.

Fu-hao noiselessly entered his office and announced that the city's headman had come to petition the court.

Lu quickly changed into his colorful, official robes with his badge of office boldly embroidered on the front. He picked up a black, gauze hat with large round flaps on either side and, after carefully placing it on his head, went into court.

Once seated behind a highly carved desk on a raised dais, he ordered the petitioner to come forward.

The man moved down the center of the hall, with a firm, yet rigid, step. He stopped before the Judge and bowed.

"What is the case you are bringing before the court?" Judge Lu asked.

"Honorable Sir, I am sorry to trouble you about this case, the death of a local farmer," he said, the corners of his mouth twitching.

Lu wondered at his nervousness. As the local headman, he must be accustomed to bringing the more serious cases to court. The lesser cases he could handle himself.

"Did you write a report and submit it to Secretary Lu Fu-hao?" Judge Lu asked.

"Yes, sir, as required. But this case involves farmer Chou."

Lu frowned. "Chou, the farmer who died accidently? Explain."

"Honorable Sir, although his death at first appeared accidental, for the past three nights a Demon has been harrowing my town."

"A Demon?" Lu asked.

The headman nodded. "Many people saw him. Every night, at the drumming of each watch, he appears with long hair flying, wearing a conical, straw hat and mourning clothing. He shakes doors and windows and has been seen on the road. Whenever anyone dares to investigate further, he disappears. Truly, he's a Demon!"

"Exactly where was he seen?" Judge Lu asked.

"He's been seen at Chou's death site and around He Qi-feng's house," the headman said. "He's angry about farmer Chou's death," he firmly added.

"Why would he appear at He Qi-feng's home?"

"He Qi-feng was helpful in taking care of a couple of problems concerning Chou's death. He put up the money for Chou's burial ceremonies, which because of his violent death included special, elaborate rites and, therefore, was expensive."

"So? The netherworld should be happy at such a magnanimous gesture," Lu said. He glanced aside and wondered why the headman was bringing the case to his court. It was neither a civil nor criminal matter and should more properly be taken to a Taoist priest.

The headman rocked from foot to foot. "Yes. Well, in return for paying for Chou's funeral, Qi-feng is buying his field—at a very low price."

"Not many people are willing to work such bad-luck land, much less buy it," Lu said.

"For some that is true." He thrust his chin out and added, "He's also taking the widow Chen as his concubine."

Lu tugged on his ear. "I see."

The headman nodded. "Perhaps, farmer Chou's ghost is angry and jealous." He scowled and shook his head. "Of course, the question is: Why?"

"As Qi-feng's concubine, Chou's wife wouldn't starve and the land wouldn't go fallow. A package deal, of sorts. How can a woman farm by herself?" Lu adjusted his position in his chair and added another real concern to himself: such an arrangement would keep Chou's wife from becoming another indigent widow and a problem to the village.

The headman's lips turned down in a frown. "Qi-feng is known to have a bad temper, so being his concubine is not necessarily the best of fates. Yet." He patted his chest. "I am sure there are other men who would even take her as a second wife." He paused, then went on more forcefully. "The Demon's coming tells us there's something wrong, something which needs to be addressed. As our magistrate, I beg you to look into this."

"If it's a Demon, why haven't you enlisted the services of an exorcist to placate farmer Chou's spirit and make the evil spirit go away?" Judge Lu asked.

"We have, Your Honor. We brought in a Taoist priest. After connecting with Chou's spirit in the netherworld, the priest told us we must investigate the death more thoroughly. Chen died too soon and he should have had a descendent. He wants justice." The headman again spoke with certainty.

Lu knew the elderly man wanted what was best for his community. They had a Demon harassing the town; plus, there was no telling what Chou's ghost would do if it felt abandoned. Right now the Demon rattled windows and doors, but Demons and ghosts were known to lead people to their deaths, to destroy homes, and cause calamities for entire villages.

"Tonight's the fourth night," the headman pulled at a large mole on his chin. "People are afraid someone will die; they're demanding action."

Lu nodded. The words *four* and *death* were homophonous, pronounced exactly the same, making the number 4 very unlucky. Tonight's being the fourth night would naturally make people anxious. He glanced at the large statue at the entrance to his courtroom. The multi-animal *Xie Zhi,* with its head of a dragon, horn of a stag, and eye of a lion, stood as a reminder of what the courts meant to the people. It was a symbol of fairness, righteousness, and justice.

Spread his fingers wide and wiping his hands in a cleansing motion over the top of his desk, Lu said, "I'll look into the matter."

After the village headman left the court, Judge Lu crafted a letter to Magistrate Yu Jiao and had his personal guard, Ma, deliver it immediately. Lu hoped to have a reply by late afternoon. Next, he sent his second trusted guard, Zhang, to bring in everyone who had surrounded the body on the pathway. Lu would interrogate each one. If, in accordance with the law, any suspicious person was not forthcoming, he'd have his jailers apply their own persuasive techniques. But he wanted to avoid such torture if possible. He wasn't squeamish; he just didn't believe torture always produced honest information. He knew some would confess to crimes they didn't commit to stop the torture's unbearable pain. He was looking for truth, if that was possible.

Qi-feng was first. When he was brought in, he appeared pale and drawn compared to the confident, in-control man Lu had first met only three days ago. Today, puffy, sleepless eyes looked out of a drawn, tense face. His responses to Lu's questions sounded mechanical and flat.

After a lackluster, short description of finding Chou's body strewn across the path, Lu wanted to push him further. "Tell me why the Demon comes to your house," Lu demanded as he slapped the desk.

At the sharp sound, Qi-feng blanched and shrank inside himself.

"I was only trying to help out a fellow farmer by buying

his worthless land," he whined, rubbing his neck with his left hand.

Judge Lu picked up a map from his desk and shook it. "Farmer Chou's land is in the best part of the valley; yours is on the hillside. How can you call his land worthless?"

"Land is only as good as the farmer," Qi-feng retorted. He straightened his shoulders and seemed to rally.

"And his wife, were you only helping there, too?" Lu thundered.

Qi-feng quivered. But he responded, saying, "Why not? She's young and already a widow. My offer's fair. If you've heard otherwise, the teller's merely trying to cause trouble. Perhaps he wants Chou's widow for himself."

Lu stared down at Qi-feng. Certainly, the circumstances seemed suspicious. He was the one to find the body and, due to Chou's death, he was prospering by gaining both productive land and a beautiful concubine. Lu shifted in his chair. How was he going to determine whether Qi-feng came into such good fortune through mere opportunism or murder? Torture might elicit a truthful confession but—Lu caressed the badge of office on his chest—if Qi-feng was innocent, the torture could cripple him for life. Lu continued to examine the defiant man kneeling before him.

"You may go, but be warned: if you are hiding anything, I will find out." With that, he released Qi-feng.

Judge Lu interviewed each of the other men present the morning of Chou's death; they had come upon the scene late and could add nothing. As for the Demon, they all agreed the phantom figure came to avenge Chou's murder. From their testimony it was clear to Judge Lu that the town was in a near state of panic. No one was sure how or where the Demon would strike, but they were sure something bad was about to happen.

Finally, Zhang led in the wizened, old woman. Her loose,

unkempt hair and unnaturally bright eyes made him wonder at her sanity. She did a half-kowtow and remained on her knees, moving her head rhythmically from side to side. While she appeared disengaged, Lu noticed she also seemed to take everything in. Carefully observing her, he wondered if she were playing a game.

"State your name, relation to the deceased, and whatever you can about the day you and the others found farmer Chou's body," Judge Lu ordered.

"Widow Han, maternal aunt to farmer Chou's wife," she said, her answers came measured and succinct. "Qi-feng was already near farmer Chou's body when I arrived. The other men came along after me. They were on the way to morning market. Qi-feng sent one of them to get the headman."

"What were you doing out on the path so early in the morning?"

"I was on my way to collect herbs for my niece, farmer Chou's wife. She wasn't feeling well."

"Chou was already dead when you arrived? Describe what you saw."

"My nephew lay partially stretched over the path. He never moved. Qi-feng stood above him, gripping his hand."

"Gripping his hand?"

"As if to pull him out of the field," she said.

Moving on, Lu asked, "And what do you know of the Demon that's been hounding the town?"

"He's not 'hounding the town,' only the guilty party," she said with a tinge of bitterness.

"Guilty party? Guilty of what? Who's guilty?" Lu's questions came in quick succession.

"Qi-feng killed Chou!" she burst out and leaped up, pepper-and-salt hair flying. "He's an evil man!" Her eyes darted around the room as if searching for something. "Chou

37

and his wife must have justice. Qi-feng must account for what he did."

Zhang moved toward Widow Han when she sprang up, ready to grab her if she attacked Lu.

"Is that what the Taoist said is needed to appease Chou's ghost?" Lu said, watching her closely. "Have you seen the Demon?"

With a grim smile, she said, "Do you doubt its reality? Ask anyone, they've all seen it, and it demands a reckoning." She looked him straight in the eyes. "Demons do not appear without cause; they come because of a grave wrong. A soul in Hell is angry or wounded by the acts of men." She pointed her dagger-like finger at Lu. "It's your duty to see justice is done."

Her antics didn't move him, but he wondered at her belligerency. Chen was family, her niece's husband. She was unlikely to be involved in his death. But then what? What did she know? What was she hiding? After a few more demands from her, and realizing he wasn't going to get any more than a deranged tirade, he let her go.

After dinner, during which Lu discussed the affair with Fu-hao and his trusted guards, Zhang and Ma, Lu brought Qi-feng back into court for further interrogation.

"Tonight's the fourth night," Lu said quietly to Qi-feng's bent figure standing before him. "The Demon will most certainly come to seek revenge against the murderer."

Qi-feng turned from a whitish pallor to a sickly gray. His shoulders slumped and he appeared to melt into the floor.

"It would be better for you to confess now before the court, rather than wait for the Demon to wreak justice upon you tonight," Lu said. He couldn't prove Qi-feng had killed

Chou, but he showed signs of extreme stress and anxiety, making Lu certain the man either knew something about the death he wasn't revealing or was himself the murderer. Right now, Lu's only tool was fear, fear of the Demon—and the power of the unknown—to push Qi-feng into telling the truth.

At first, Qi-feng didn't move or speak; then he slowly sat up from his kneeling position and stared at Judge Lu with haunted eyes. Lu let silence fill the space between them.

Finally, as if deciding the human court was preferable to the court of the dead, Qi-feng said, "Chou was nothing, yet he had good land. I have more land, but it's not as fertile. There's no way for me to prosper with what I have."

He smirked. "And then, when I saw Chou's new wife, I thought, *Why not take her, too? She's a beauty and he's a useless fool.*" He looked up at Lu. "That's when I knew I had to have both the land and the woman. Chou had to die."

Judge Lu thoughtfully studied Qi-feng. "You are the foolish one," he said and arrested Qi-feng for the murder of farmer Chou.

———

Later, Ma returned with a response from Magistrate Yu Jiao. Lu had investigated Chou's wound as thoroughly as his expertise allowed, but he felt he needed assistance from the more knowledgeable Magistrate Yu. Thus, he'd sent Yu Jiao a detailed description of Chou's wounds: broken bones on his face around his right eye and a knife wound on his abdomen.

Grateful for the quick response, Lu opened Magistrate Yu's letter and carefully read through it. Yu Jiao wrote that if the knife wound had caused the death, Lu would have found signs of bleeding in the area around the wound and blood on the ground. If the head wound had been the reason for death, and the body was cut with the sickle later, there wouldn't be much, if any, blood from the knife wound, depending on how much time had passed. Given the description Lu sent, it appeared to Yu that the abdominal cut was administered after death. Further, he noted, it would take a powerful blow to cause the damage found to the bones around the eyes. Merely hitting some rocks with his face as he fell would not crush the bones in the way Lu had described. Finally, the broken bones on the right side indicated a left-handed killer.

Judge Lu took out his notebook on "Essential Points for Examination at Death" and copied Yu Jiao's comments into it. With He Qi-feng's confession and Magistrate Yu Jiao's analysis, Lu was confident he'd found farmer Chou's murderer.

Leaning back in his chair, he thought of a couplet the great first Ming Emperor wrote:

With one blow of the hands,
The road to life and death is cleft open;
With one stroke of the knife
The root of right and wrong is cut off.

Lu rested his hand upon his notebook. He'd learned something new in this case, something which would help him in the future—when he couldn't count on a Demon to come to his assistance.

Originally published as "Reckoning, from Judge Lu's Ming Dynasty Case Files" in the online magazine *Kings River Life* (2014): http://kingsriverlife.com/11/29/reckoning-a-mystery-short-story/.

CHAPTER 4
THE IMMORTALITY MUSHROOM

J udge Lu enjoyed his visits to the Temple of the Enduring Oak. He'd discovered a sympathetic soul in its head monk, Tsu Fei-long. When possible, Lu would slip away from his duties in order to enjoy a cup of tea and the pleasure of an afternoon filled with philosophical discussion. Such visits provided him with relief from his busy and stressful schedule as magistrate of the local province.

Today, however, they had just begun their discussion when a monk entered the room and whispered in Tsu Fei-long's ear. Fei-long nodded and glanced at Lu. "Come with me, Your Honor. There is something you need to see." His tone was solemn.

They followed the young monk out of the temple, past the massive oak the temple was named after, and to the nearby river. As they walked by, Lu's eyes lingered for a moment on the giant oak. Because of its age and size, the temple's namesake represented longevity and was, therefore, respected as a good luck omen.

Two saffron-robed monks were on the banks directing a young fellow who strode hip deep into the river. He skimmed the water's surface with a net. A cry went up when he snagged something and started dragging it toward shore.

By the time Lu and Fei-long reached the trio, one of the monks cradled the object in his arms. Bending, he gently laid it on a square piece of cloth draped on the grassy bank. Lu recognized a tiny, puffy body covered unevenly with reddish blotches. He turned his head and closed his eyes against the sight. A drowned newborn.

Fei-long spoke quietly to his monks. They wrapped the body and carried it up the slight hill.

"You can examine it in the shade of the temple," he said to Lu. As they turned to go, he added, "That's the second little one we've found this month."

Lu frowned. "The second?" Why hadn't he been told?

Before he could ask, however, Fei-long said, "We find several every year. Their parents, too poor to feed another mouth, drown them rather than have everyone else in the family suffer even more deprivation, possibly even threatening the lives of their other children."

"It was a girl child," Lu said, a statement, not a question.

Fei-long sucked in his breadth. "Yes. We rarely find a boy child. Boys are too precious, even in times of want."

Lu nodded. Girls were expendable. They grew up to marry and become a part of someone else's family, to help carry on their line. Boys, on the other hand, were essential to the survival of the family and to maintaining the family line. He knew the families didn't make these decisions easily, but in making the decision of which child to abandon, there was no choice. The family line must survive.

Pu-an was a large district. Most of its citizens had enough to eat and a good percentage were even well off. However, there were always those families on the margins. The working poor and the abject poor. He knew it was useless to go looking for the infant's parents. No one would say anything;

no one would know anything. Infanticide was a moral quagmire, but he also recognized the monk was right: the cause was not callousness or uncaring parents. The crime rose from fear of want, of hopelessness, of true poverty.

Riding back to the yamen with his two personal guards, Ma and Zhang, Lu thought about the temple giving each of the little victims a burial. As magistrate, he was called father of the people. As their symbolic father, it was his job to keep the citizens safe. But how could he eliminate the killing of innocent babies?

Deep in thought, he rode through the town unaware of the merchants' calls and the excited bargaining voices of buyers and sellers. He ignored it all as he rounded the last corner and the yamen's massive, wooden gate rose majestically ahead of him, drawing him in.

"Sir! Honorable Sir!" A high-pitched voice rose above the street's cacophony.

Zhang, coming from behind Lu, immediately thrust out his spear and urged his horse forward. The woman—arms flailing and her loose, untamed hair flying—ignored Zhang and continued rushing toward the judge. Ma moved closer, placing his horse between Lu and the wild figure.

Lu, however, instantly recognized her as Widow Han from a previous case. He pushed thoughts of the drowned babies away and concentrated on this new development. He told his guards to let her pass.

Breathing rapidly, she stopped within an arm's distance of his horse. She paused, hand on her chest, gasping for air.

Lifting a worn, wrinkled face toward him, she said, "Your Honor, Master Chou is dead. Someone robbed and killed him."

Lu scowled down at her. "Master Chou? Who is he and where did this happen?"

"He's the bell doctor who lives on Dong Jie," she said,

referring to the itinerant doctor by the local term. He walked the streets ringing a bell, alerting people to his presence in case they needed his services. "I went to visit. I came at the very moment his son found him dead in their house."

"Lead us to Master Chou's," Lu ordered the widow.

She didn't hesitate or turn to see if they were following as she sped back through the streets; she moved at a surprising speed, belying her fragile, if erratic, appearance. Lu pushed himself to keep up.

A crowd had already started to form around the bell doctor's door. A strongly-built man of medium height, with small eyes and prematurely thinning hair, stood just inside the house and kept the onlookers at bay.

The throng parted as Lu and his entourage approached, allowing Widow Han to stride straight up to the intimidating man. "Chou Wen-zei, I've brought Magistrate Lu," she said loudly.

He scowled down at her, but then, as he watched the judge dismount from his horse, the frown passed. "Honorable Sir," Wen-zei said while bowing in Lu's direction, "please come in."

As he stepped through the doorway, Lu immediately found himself wrapped in a pungent gloom. He paused and looked around, letting his eyes become accustomed to the room's dimness. Shelves overflowing with jars and bottles stretched along two walls. In the center stood a long table with three stools pushed under it. A second table, this one small and square, filled out the remaining space. On the latter, Lu noted a cutting board, chopping knife, and mortar and pestle resting on its rough, work-worn surface. Master Chou's body lay stretched out on the long table, a light cloth covering him.

Lu wanted to be mindful of the pain and shock he was sure Master Chou's son was feeling at his father's sudden and horrible death. Nevertheless, it was imperative he proceed as quickly as possible, before details were forgotten or altered.

Plus, and this he tried to ignore because it could lead to inefficiency and subvert impartiality, Lu was also too keenly aware that—as a magistrate—his superiors expected him to discover and apprehend the murderer within days of the death. Anything less than this and the magistrate was suspected of mishandling the case; there would be repercussions. Perhaps even dismissal.

Lu tried not to let such thoughts determine his actions. He concentrated on bringing justice to the victims, not on protecting his own position.

He stepped to the table and pulled back the cover. At the same time as he bent to inspect the body, he was aware of Widow Han's slipping into room and taking up a position behind the open door. He ignored her, allowing her to remain. Looking at the body, the cause of death was immediately apparent: a bashed-in skull. No other signs of trauma were visible on the body.

"Where did you find him?" Lu asked Chou Wen-zei.

"There," he said pointing to a narrow space between the long table and the shelves.

"He was already dead?"

Wen-zei passed a hand over his eyes. "Yes. I was bringing in fire wood and found him slumped over on the floor. He didn't have to die like that. A violent death."

"Did he have any enemies? Anyone he was fighting with?"

"No. No one I knew. Of course, he was a doctor and sometimes people died, no matter what he did to save them. Sometimes families blamed him. But I don't know of anyone who'd kill him."

Lu glanced around the room, "Was anything stolen?"

"Nothing."

Lu heard a sharp intake of breath from Widow Han, but

he didn't glance in her direction. "Are you sure? There are a lot of jars around here. Are you certain none are missing?"

"I work with my father. I know everything in this room. Nothing's missing."

"Did he have any appointments today?"

"Not that I know of. As I said, I was out fetching wood, so if anyone stopped in, I wouldn't know it. But I don't think he had any appointments. He was preparing his medicines."

After closely inspecting the room, Lu again returned to the body. Suppressing his own sense of revulsion, he gently moved his fingers through Master Chou's matted hair, feeling the skull's wound in more detail. His job was to carry out a thorough investigation, and he would do it to the best of his abilities.

The late afternoon sun sent a sliver of light through the small window, highlighting the bloodied mass. As he pushed the hair out of the way, he felt a few chunks of matter. He picked them out, wrapping them in a handkerchief, and placed the evidence in his sleeve. Continuing to carefully feel around the wound, he noted the point of impact was rounded, not long and narrow.

Lu glanced around the room once more. His eyes rested on the pestle used for pounding herbs and such into powders. He picked it up and gently held it close to the victim's wound. The pestle was clean, but it matched the injury.

Wen-zei watched Lu. "Do you think that's what killed him?"

Wrapping the pestle in another handkerchief, Lu handed it to his guard. "Very likely."

"A thief came in and killed my father, thinking he could rob him. But we never had any money here." He smiled grimly. "Bell doctors don't make much."

Lu ran his hand over the table's rough surface, dislodging a couple of pieces of vegetable matter from its crevices. He put those into another handkerchief and dropped them gently into his sleeve along with the first handkerchief.

Back in his office, Lu sat with his brother Lu Fu-hao, who was also his secretary, and his two guards. They discussed Master Chou's death. The killing seemed random; there was no motive and no suspect. Yet, such a violent murder suggested a degree of passion. But from what? Fear? Anger? Desperation? The fact that Master Chou had his back turned toward the killer indicated he wasn't afraid of him. Perhaps he even knew his killer and trusted him. Lu was certain it wasn't a woman because of the strength required for such a blow to crush the skull.

As they sat sifting through the scant information Lu had gathered that afternoon, his servant announced Widow Han was outside, requesting an audience.

Lu slipped on his court robes and returned to his desk.

Widow Han wandered into the room. Not for the first time, Lu wondered at her mercurial behavior. She appeared to go from aggressive assertiveness to mistily drifting in and out of consciousness. Watching her, he wondered at her sanity. He sighed and waited.

When she arrived at the desk, she stopped and looked around her as if surprised to find herself in the office. She cocked her head to one side and—as if continuing a conversation—said, "You know, Master Chou also talked to that farmer from the eastern hillside. Farmer Xiong. The one who comes to town to sell vegetables on market day at the stall across the street from him."

Lu and Fu-hao exchanged glances.

"When did Chou talk to the farmer?" Lu asked.

"The same day he found the mushrooms." She glanced

around the room. "He might have told the farmer about the mushrooms. He told me." She stopped and stared up at Lu.

He shifted his weight in his elaborate high-backed chair. "And what is it that he told you?"

"Why, that he'd found them, of course. Although I suppose it would have been better for him not to mention anything to anyone. Not even me." She shook her head and bit her lip.

Lu cast another look at Fu-hao who was sitting at a side table, taking notes on the meeting. Fu-hao caught his glance, widened his eyes, and shook his head in silent comment on her behavior. Lu shifted back into place.

"Are you saying he'd found mushrooms? That's what he told you and the other farmer?" He wondered how finding mushrooms could be so interesting or require secrecy.

Widow Han looked up, eyes bright. "Yes. The Immortality Mushroom."

Startled, Lu stared at the woman. Had he heard correctly?

She hurriedly went on as if she had to get the whole event out. "I met him on my way back to town. I'd been out gathering herbs, just as he had been. He was looking for lichen and mushrooms in the woods—the one with a stand of old oak trees in it." She licked her lips. "And there they were— three of them—growing on the side of an oak stump."

"Are you sure? How did he recognize them? The Immortality Mushroom is extremely rare."

Shifting from side to side in a rhythmic sway, she smiled. "Rare, yes. The golden treasure. Any herbalist would be able to identify one; they are distinctive with their bright red color and broad, flat shape. Even one would bring a lifetime of wealth. It's what we all hope to find as we go about our hunt for herbs. And, Master Chou found three!" She smiled as if in awe at his luck. "He was so excited. When he saw me on the road, he had to tell me the whole story of his looking for lichens, of finding the mushrooms. While he was telling me the tale, Farmer Xiong came along. I warned Master Chou not to say anything more. He was walking around with a treasure and anyone could steal it."

She held Judge Lu's gaze. "But I think Farmer Xiong had heard enough to know Master Chou had something of great value."

"Do you think he knew it was the mushrooms?" Lu asked.

She shook her head. "No, probably not. And he wouldn't recognize the importance of the mushrooms—at least I don't think so. Who really knows what someone else knows?"

"When was this?"

"Four days ago. I went by his place today because I was sure he would have prepared the mushrooms for sale by now, drying them and grinding them into a powder."

"Wouldn't he sell them whole, so the customer could be assured he was getting a real Immortality Mushroom?" Lu asked.

"They are too powerful. They need to be mixed in with special vegetables and longevity noodles and eaten over several days."

Lu fingered the tiny, dried chunks he'd taken from the wound and then laid his hand on Master Chou's pestle. "Look at these, Widow Han. What do you think they are?"

She stepped up to the desk, pressed her nose close to the pieces, and sniffed. Lifting her head slightly, she studied them and turned them over with her index finger. "Immortality Mushrooms," she said with conviction.

Lu pushed his shoulders back and stared down at the fragments. "So, he might have been grinding the mushrooms when he was struck down." They didn't look like much to him, just brown and reddish bits, nothing worth murdering for. "The killer must have known how valuable they were. The table and mortar were thoroughly cleaned."

Crinkling her wizened features, she nodded at the bits on his desk. "Even those few pieces are worth a half a year's wages."

"Thank you, Widow Han. You have been most helpful," he said and was about to dismiss her when she said, "One more thing, Your Honor."

He inclined his head, indicating she could continue.

"Chou Wen-zei must have known about the mushrooms. I doubt his father could have kept such great luck from his son. Yet, he said nothing was missing."

"Yes. It's possible Master Chou was killed for other reasons and then, when his son found him, he hid the precious mushrooms to sell later." He pursed his lips in thought.

"No insult intended Your Honor, but he could be hiding them in order to protect his wealth when this case goes to court."

He grimaced. She was right. Once a case came to court, bribery was rife at every level, from those who wrote the required court affidavits to those who delivered the documents. The victim and his family also had to pay for protection of their home against theft and vigilante violence. The amount of bribery exacted at each and every level depended on how much money people thought the victim's family had. Hiding such newfound wealth would be reasonable. Master Chou's son could easily be penniless by the end of the trial.

Lu spun toward his personal guards. "Ma, bring in Farmer Xiong immediately for questioning. Zhang, I want you to go to Master Chou's neighborhood and talk to everyone you can. Find out who might have gone into his house or who was nearby. Find out if there was any gossip about his having these valuable mushrooms. Report back as soon as you can."

Early the next morning, Judge Lu sat behind his official court desk. His soldiers lined each side of the room. Fu-hao, as court recorder, sat at a table on the side and behind the soldiers. A dark, dense liquid filled his inkstone, and his brush rested in his hand perpendicular to the rice paper. He was ready to take notes of the interrogation.

"Farmer Xiong," a young man in a dark robe announced from the back of the court. Almost immediately, a burly soldier led in a lean man of medium height. His plain, short jacket worn over pants, which were gathered below the knees by wrapping, indicated he was a laborer or a farmer. With wide, staring eyes and hunched shoulders, he kept bowing even before he reached the front of the court.

Lu watched him come forward with satisfaction. The farmer was clearly terrified and overwhelmed. Lu was confident this would ensure a more honest response in the inquisition.

"You were on the road four days ago and met with Master Chou and Widow Han. Tell me everything about that meeting," Lu ordered.

Farmer Xiong had grasped his hands so tightly together that his knuckles were a shiny pallid color. "Yes Sir. As I came down the road, I saw Master Chou talking excitedly with Widow Han."

"You know the Widow Han?"

"Yes, Sir. Everyone knows her. She's taken care of most folks' families at one time or another, same as Master Chou."

"Go on," Lu said.

"I'd never seen Master Chou so stirred up. He's an honorable man, quiet. That day he was almost hopping in the street, waving a bag around. Widow Han was laughing and seemed to be congratulating him."

"Did they tell you what he was so happy about?"

Farmer Xiong frowned. "No. When they saw me coming

up to them, they both stopped. It was as if they were hiding something. I said hello and they said hello but they obviously didn't want me to hear what they were talking about."

"What did you do?"

"Me?" He shrugged. "I went on my way. I had a load of vegetables to sell and the sooner I got to market, the sooner I'd go home."

Lu observed the lanky farmer as he went through his description. Although he was clearly nervous at being in court, he showed no signs of being disingenuous or hiding information. Unless he was extremely clever and an adept liar, Lu believed him to be no more than he appeared: a simple man giving simple, honest answers.

After releasing Farmer Xiong, Lu returned to his office with Fu-hao and Ma. Waiting impatiently for Zhang to return, he hoped his guard had discovered something useful. How could a man be robbed and killed without anyone knowing about it?

He tried to divert his attention by going over old files from his predecessor, familiarizing himself with cases involving chronic small-time criminals. Having a list of names of such people would help him in future cases. They could either provide him with insider knowledge of the district's underworld or with the beginning of a list of possible criminals for new cases.

As he went through the documents, the name Chou Wen-zei caught his eye more than once. He'd been involved in a couple of rowdy situations where the police had to come and arrest the combatants. He'd also been arrested once for theft, but his father compensated the victim and Wen-zei was let off with a beating.

Hum. So Master Chou's son had a history of violence and theft. Interesting. Lu was considering the possible implications of Wen-zei's violent history when he saw Zhang step inside the office door.

"Good. You're here. Come and tell us what you've discovered," Lu said, waving toward a chair next to his brother Fuhao and Ma.

As Lu's servant poured tea for everyone, Zhang tucked his large frame onto the sturdy chair. He sat straight as if at attention.

"Everyone I talked to respected the doctor. He'd helped most of them and was known for his generosity. He'd care for those who couldn't afford to pay or could only make partial payments. He always said he was building merit. No matter how I asked it, no one indicated they knew anything about his finding the Immortality Mushrooms or even having anything of value. It seems Master Chou managed to keep his treasure a secret."

"How about his son, Wen-zei," Lu asked.

Zhang's lips thinned into a frown. "Now that's another story entirely," he said. "Almost to a man, they agreed that the son, from the time he was a young man, was the bane of Master Chou's life. Chou's wife managed to keep the peace between her husband and son when she was alive, but when she died two years ago, the relationship between them became even more strained. Master Chou had trained his son to be a bell doctor, but because of his violent reputation and thievery, people didn't trust him. Finally, Chou threw Wen-zei out of the house about a year ago."

"And yet, he was there, at the house, yesterday," Lu said.

"Perhaps he was trying to reunite with his father," Ma said. "Wen-zei did say he'd brought wood for him."

Lu nodded. He drummed his fingertips on the table while he ran over yesterday in his mind. Finally, he asked, "Do any of you remember seeing a load of wood in Master Chou's room?"

They all shook their heads. Zhang added, "I'd peeked in the back room as well, in case there was anyone hiding there. There were only a couple of sticks near the stove."

"Zhang, Ma, arrest Chou Wen-zei. Don't bring him to court; take him directly to jail and place him under the head jailer's care."

The two men nodded and strode from the room.

"Is that wise?" Fu-hao asked. "You know what the head jailer will do."

"Yes. He'll threaten torture unless Wen-zei can pay him off," Lu said leaning back in his glossy, ornately carved, wood chair. He sipped his tea and then held the cup up, examining the porcelain's luminescent design.

Fu-hao grinned. "Ah, yes. To get the bribe, Wen-zei will have to get one of his cronies to sell some of the Immortality Mushroom. He'll lead us right to them. Proving he stole the mushrooms," Fu-hao said, then muttered, "and implicating himself in his father's death."

Lu sadly nodded. "The most serious and monstrous crime anyone can commit: patricide."

"How could he have done such a thing?" Fu-hao asked. But they both knew there was no answer. The crime was too overwhelming, too horrific. It was against all the rules of nature. "He deserves to be tortured," Fu-hao added, anger tingeing his voice.

Two days later, Lu had Wen-zei brought before the court. Most of the people living in Master Chou's neighborhood were in the back of the room, ready to hear the proceedings.

Barely able to walk, two soldiers half carried Wen-zei into the hall. Large patches of sweat marred his clothing. His matted hair formed a skull cap on his head. When he raised his eyes, they were devoid of light. He was a defeated man.

Lu never liked torture. The law permitted it, expected its use. His superiors believed it was an efficient route to achieve justice. Evidence might indicate who the guilty party is, but— by law—no one could be convicted and sentenced of such a heinous crime if he did not confess. Therefore, torture was considered an important tool for producing confessions and obtaining a moral balance once more.

"Chou Wen-zei, confess to your crimes of murdering your father, Master Chou, and stealing the Immortality Mushrooms," Lu thundered.

"I..."

"Louder! So all can learn of your evil transgressions," Lu said.

Wen-zei began again. "I struck my father on the head with a pestle. It broke his skull and he died. I didn't mean to kill him. I needed money and he wouldn't help me. I knew he had the Immortality Mushrooms. He'd told me; he was so proud of it; said it would make us rich. Still, he wouldn't give me any money right then, and I needed it.

"I was so angry I didn't think about what I was doing. I just grabbed the pestle and hit him." He looked around, eyes empty. "I really didn't mean to hurt him. I was just angry."

He bent his head, then looked up again. "Once I saw he was dead, I took the mushrooms. He didn't need them anymore. I did."

Lu had Fu-hao read out Wen-zei's confession and Wen-zei put his mark on it.

———

Back in his office, Fu-hao asked his brother, "What are you going to do with Master Chou's Immortality Mushrooms?"

Lu studied his brother's face for some time before answering. "Master Chou and his wife have no other children. There is no one to take care of their spirits in the afterlife. I am going to confiscate the mushrooms and his property, which would have all gone to their son, and buy land as the basis of a foundation for an orphanage for abandoned babies.

"Poor families will not have to kill their babies; they can leave them without question at the great oak tree outside the Temple of the Enduring Oak. We'll get volunteers from our community to provide food and clothing. And we'll hire other poor women as wet nurses. The land's rent will provide a sustainable foundation for the orphanage. On Qing Ming Day and on this day every year, a great feast will be offered to Master Chou and his wife's spirits in thanks for providing life to so many newborns."

Fu-hao nodded solemnly. "Such a decision will earn you merit as well."

Lu didn't answer but bent his head as he wrote out his decision.

Originally published as "The Immortality Mushroom, from Judge Lu's Ming Dynasty Case Files," in *Murder Under the Oaks*, ed. Art Taylor (Down & Out Books, 2015) pages 11-24.

CHAPTER 5
FIREWORKS

The red silk lantern's flame glowed in the early morning darkness as Magistrate Lu and his younger brother, Fu-hao, sat in amiable silence, enjoying their breakfast. The sweet, fresh air spoke of spring. Fu-hao picked up his bowl of rice gruel and took a sip.

Without warning, a sharp explosion broke the peace. Startled, Fu-hao nearly spilled the thin white liquid onto his navy-blue robe. Brilliant sparks of light danced over the top of the yamen's courtyard wall, filling the lower sky.

"Even when we know it's coming, it's a surprise," Lu said.

"Rockets are a serious business. People shouldn't be able to shoot them off," Fu-hao groused.

Before he could continue, they were overwhelmed with short bursts surrounded by the rat-a-tat-tat of popping and crackling noises. Intense flashes of light rapidly appeared and disappeared.

"That's what I mean. Really, the Emperor should forbid rockets."

"Celebrating the monk Li Tian and his invention of

...y's fireworks shouldn't be discouraged," Lu said. "It's ...mportant to our people. The noise chases away ghosts and all that is evil, and the smoke cleanses everything. Together, they bring peace, health, and happiness."

After another round of sound and light pulsated through the courtyard, Lu sat back and added, "I only hope we don't have any fires with all this celebrating. I told the city security units to be prepared..."

"Sir," a voice called out. Ma, Lu's guard, strode into the lanterns' light. "The city headman is here."

"Send him in," Lu said.

An elderly man with a sparse beard shuffled into the room. The city headman was an elder in the community and oversaw much of the city's day-to-day activities. When problems arose, he either solved them himself or, in more serious instances, brought them to the magistrate.

Once the elder had successfully hobbled up to Lu's table, he stopped, bowed, and said, "Your honor, I have unfortunate news to relate." He paused. "The Liu brothers from Hunan province have a shop on Shan Di road. An apparently successful shop."

"And? What's the problem?" Lu asked.

"There has been an accident. Most inauspicious. Especially today. Most inauspicious."

"Yes?"

"I have to report that very early this morning, when the Liu brothers were setting off fireworks, something went amiss. A rocket exploded, instantly killing the elder brother, Liu Shih-kuei." He finished with his words tumbling over each other as though even speaking them would heighten the evil of such a death.

Lu and his entourage of Fu-hao, as court secretary, and Ma and Zhang, his personal guards, rode through the tumultuous streets to the Liu brothers' shop. The ferocity of firecrackers erupted all along their route. Smoke enveloped them, cutting off their air and stinging their eyes. Children ran laughing from one cascading pandemonium to the next. Lu worked to sooth his fearful horse as it tried to escape the gauntlet of noise.

In spite of the bedlam, Lu's mind never veered far from the scene he feared would greet them: a body mutilated by a rocket. His stomach churned and bile rose in his throat. He tightened the horse's reins.

They soon arrived at a weathered building with a multi-layered tree of spent firecrackers leaning against its wall. A clerk appeared, solemnly welcomed them, and led them into a dim back room. As Lu's eyes adjusted, he saw a beefy, sunburnt fellow lounging under the only window. Another—a thin, young man, sitting immobilized behind a tall desk—rested his hand on an abacus near a closed ledger. As Lu entered, the man looked up with eyes as hollow as empty wine cups. He appeared to be in shock. Nevertheless, when Lu approached—wearing his official robe with its large, square, magistrate's badge of office emblazoned on the chest —the young man jumped up, rounded the desk, and bowed deeply.

"Your Honor, I am Liu Shih-hua, owner of this establish-ment. It is my brother, Shih-kuei, who passed away this morning." he said and stopped, as if at a loss for words. His eyes flitted toward the window and back to the judge.

Lu glanced out the window. The early morning sun cast a long shadow over a narrow courtyard. Lone, potted trees marked each of the far corners.

A clerk brought a chair for the magistrate. Fu-hao took

over the desk, preparing to record the interview for the court's report. Ma and Zhang stood at the door.

Shih-hua first introduced the other visitor as a Mr. Rui of the Hunan Province's Merchants Association, there to help organize the burial details. Then, Shih-hua recounted the morning's drama, his voice low and deferential.

"As usual, my brother and I arrived at the shop well before daylight. Getting here early today was especially important because we wanted to set off the fireworks exactly at sunrise. He thought that would be the most propitious time for our business.

"My brother had recently returned from our hometown in Hunan and brought back the most amazing fireworks display and even a rocket." Shih-hua opened his eyes wide as if in admiration. "The fireworks display would certainly be the best we've ever had." He stopped, rubbed his eyes and shook his head. "I admit I was nervous about the rocket's safety; it made me nervous. But it's what my brother wanted and he'd bought it at a very good price. There was no way he would pass up the chance to set it off on this most auspicious day." Shih-hua linked his hands in front of him, sighing, as if aware of the irony of his last words.

"You didn't think it was too dangerous for him to ignite the rocket himself?"

Shih-hua shrugged and repeated. "It's what he wanted. He's my older brother. He decides—decided—what we should do."

Lu nodded. Of course, that was what tradition dictated, although he knew plenty of families where it was the more capable, not the oldest, who made decisions. Nevertheless, he said, "I see. Go on."

Shih-hua took a deep breath. "The clerks and I went into the street to light the firecrackers."

"Both clerks went with you? Your brother was alone?"

"The fireworks display was massive. I needed both men to help. Shih-kuei didn't need anyone; he only had one rocket.

"As I set off the fireworks I heard an explosion from inside. We rushed back, hoping to catch a glimpse of the rocket's fire and light." He frowned. "Too late, of course. I didn't realize how quickly it was over."

"And that's when you found him?"

"My brother lay on the ground, blood everywhere. The rocket was defective and exploded." Shih-hua covered his face with his hands. Recovering, he added, "I immediately sent one of the clerks to the city headman to report the accident."

Lu glanced at the large man near the window. "And you alerted the Hunan Merchant Association?"

Shih-hua nodded. "They handle the burial plans."

Nothing new there. Most merchants spent much of their time traveling and living in other cities far from their families, they join a home area association where they find other merchants from their town, city, or province. These associations provided both a wide range of practical benefits, such as a temporary place to stay, a ready pool of friendship, and at times credit or a job, if needed. It was a particularly important network for a sojourner who finds himself living among strangers.

"Why did your brother go home?" Lu asked.

"He went to celebrate his second son's one-year birthday. I stayed here because we couldn't afford to close the shop."

"How long was he gone?"

"Three months."

"Isn't that a long time?"

"I was here; he didn't have to hurry. I could take care of the shop, and he wanted to spend time with his wife and children."

"Are you married?" Lu asked.

Shih-hua clasped his hands together and said, "I have a wife but no children as yet. She lives with my parents and cares for them."

"Where does your older brother's family live?"

"With my parents." Shih-hua looked him straight in the eyes. "We are a strong family. We live together and work together. As is proper," he finished.

He examined the young man before him. The large family, which consisted of married brothers, their wives, and children living together with the elderly parents in one household, was the ideal. However, the real-life pressures of sharing responsibilities and resources equally, not to mention the clash of personalities, often made such a household arrangement difficult to impossible. He wondered how closely the Liu family actually fit the ideal.

"You can be commended on your family's virtue," Lu said.

"Thank you, Your Honor," Shih-hua said, head down, hands clasped in a white knuckled grip.

Out under the courtyard's veranda, a covered body lay on a slab of wood. Blood splatters told Lu where he died. A table and chairs for the judge and his secretary had been set up on the surrounding wooden porch, outside the bloodied area. After Fu-hao had arranged his writing implements and taken a seat, Lu approached the body and turned back the cloth. As he feared, the body was badly burned with multiple injuries.

At Lu's order, Ma removed the corpse's tattered clothing. Taking a knife, Lu paused and took a deep breath before proceeding. This was something he was sure he'd never get used to. But, he had no choice. It was his job.

After another long breath, he dug into several of the

wounds and extracted iron pellets and broken pieces of porcelain. He placed each item into a sheet of paper, folded it, and placed it into a small pouch, which he dropped into his voluminous sleeve.

Glad to have that part of his job over, he stretched and looked away from the body. After studying the courtyard's walls and porch columns, he walked to the area closest to where the rocket was detonated. A pattern of small holes spread across the wall. Again, using his knife, he dug into the wood and removed more iron balls and bits of porcelain. As with the first bits, he collected them for analysis and as documentation of the tragedy.

Standing with hands behind his back, he looked over the enclosed, bare patch of dirt. He reconstructed the early morning scene: Shih-kuei alone when he set off the rocket; the others out front, preparing the firecracker display.

Running his fingers over the holes in the wall and posts, he noted their pattern.

"This was no celebratory rocket," he said to Fu-hao. "It was a bomb, disguised as a rocket and designed to mutilate and kill. It came from a military arsenal."

Fu-hao paused, his brush resting on the inkstone. "How could a merchant get such a thing?"

Lu slowly made his way around the veranda, looking for areas where the bomb's contents had struck. He stopped at the table, silent, lost in thought.

"We'll need to interrogate everyone," Lu said. "Ma, bring the clerk who attended Liu Shih-kuei on his trip to Hunan."

Lu settled in the chair on the veranda near Fu-hao, facing out into the courtyard's neglected space.

A shaken, middle-aged man entered and stood on the bare ground below Lu. He bowed.

"I am Clerk Hao, and have been serving the Liu family for more than twenty years. I started under their father,

Master Liu, and later worked for his sons when Master Liu retired."

"Have you always worked here in the city of Pu-an, in Jiangxi province, or did you work in a city in Hunan Province?"

"When I clerked under Master Liu, he had a shop in Pu-an but not here," his lips turned down. "Master Liu had a large building on the main road. His sons had to move to this small shop on Xiao Lu road last year."

"Was there a problem with the business?" Lu asked.

The clerk nodded. "The brothers had to move or close their business entirely."

Lu pursed his lips in thought. "What happened? Our town is prosperous and the original shop was in a good area. What caused their business to have such bad luck?"

The clerk shuffled from one foot to another, then said, "As the oldest son, Shih-kuei ran the business. Unfortunately, he had many debts and spent most of their profits." He again shifted his weight and glanced away.

"How?" Lu asked.

"Shih-kuei had expensive habits; he caroused and was well known at the brothels. He was rarely here. Shih-hua takes care of the everyday business, but it's like a minnow swimming upstream."

Lu continued, "Do you know where Shih-kuei bought the rocket?"

"No. I didn't know he had one. He bought a large fire-cracker display, but I don't know about the rocket. I thought they made him nervous. But...maybe he wanted extra good luck for their business this year."

Bad choice, Lu thought.

After the clerk left, Lu ordered Ma to bring in the second clerk.

A boy just reaching his manhood stepped into the courtyard. His round face had little color and his eyes darted around and finally halted at Lu's chest, fixating on the brilliantly colored magistrate's badge. He bowed low and deep.

"I am Clerk Tsai from Jiangxi province. I began apprenticing for the Liu family five months ago. This morning we started setting up to celebrate Li Tian well before daybreak."

"When did you come in?"

"I sleep at the shop, so I was here when the Liu brothers arrived."

"What do you know about the fireworks?"

"When Master Shih-kuei returned from Hunan, they stored the firecracker display in a room behind the courtyard. I never saw the rocket until today."

"Who brought the rocket in and set it up?"

The young man closed his eyes as if seeing the morning's events. "Mr. Rui brought in a large box yesterday. He and Master Shih-hua went into the back room. I heard them opening the box. I didn't hear what they said because their voices were too soft."

"Was Shih-kuei with them?"

"Master Shih-kuei was out." He cast a quick glance at the door to the shop. "He was at a wine shop yesterday and didn't return until this morning." He stopped and bit his lip as if reviewing a play. "I didn't think he would ignite the rocket because, when he found out about it this morning, he wasn't happy."

"Wasn't happy?" asked Lu.

Tsai nodded. "Master Shih-hua said they had to set it off, to improve business. They needed all the good luck they could get. There was an argument over who would ignite it. Shih-hua insisted Shih-kuei had to ignite the rocket since he was the older brother; it wouldn't be as auspicious if a younger brother did it. Eventually, Shih-kuei agreed.

"And now he's dead," the young clerk finished in a barely audible tone. "Bad luck."

When the boy left, Judge Lu ordered Mr. Rui enter for questioning.

The burly man strode into the courtyard and bowed quickly to the judge. Hard eyes looked out of a face with an intersecting set of scars on his left cheek.

"I am Rui Ren of the Hunan Province's Merchants Association. I came to the city looking for a job. I'm from Hunan but had traveled some before coming here."

"Where did you live before coming to Pu-an?" Lu asked.

Rui Ren licked his lips. "I lived in Shaanxi province for a few years. Another association member, who had also lived in Shaanxi, offered me work as the association's security guard.

"I'm acquainted with the Liu brothers through our group, that's all."

"Why are you here, at the shop?" Lu asked.

"Liu Shih-hua sent a message to the hall and I came to fulfill the association's responsibilities in assisting in the funeral rites. It's the first time I've been to their shop."

Lu leaned forward and demanded, "What about yesterday?"

Rui Ren's face twitched. He said, "I was here yesterday. I forgot. It wasn't important. I delivered a box to the shop."

"What was in the box?"

"I don't know. I simply delivered it."

"Don't lie to the court!" Lu thundered. "You were here and opened the box. If you don't tell me now, I have ways to learn the truth."

Rui Ren stared at the judge, then spat on the ground. Ma lurched forward, his staff readied to slam into Rui Ren. Lu raised a hand to stop his guard, causing Ma to halt mid-step.

"Speak!" Lu ordered.

"I brought a box to Liu Shih-hua yesterday," he began

sullenly. "Someone, I don't know who, left it at the association's hall with a note to deliver it to the Lius' shop. I didn't know what was in it until Shih-hua opened the box. It was a rocket. That wasn't a surprise; a lot of people are setting off rockets today. I didn't think anything of it."

As if to corroborate his story, the courtyard throbbed with another round of sharp bursts. Lu ignored them.

"Tell the court about your military experience."

At this, Rui started, eyes wide. "How did... Alright. Yes, I had a small problem with the law and was sentenced to military duty for six years, stationed on the Shaanxi border."

"And that's where you had access to rockets and bombs."

Rui Ren began to spit again, glanced at Ma with his staff, and swallowed. "I did my time and came back to Hunan, but people don't forget the past. I eventually came to Pu-an and settled here. The only person I told about my military experience is the fellow who helped me find a job with the association."

"What about Shih-hua?" Lu asked.

"Shih-hua is married to my sister."

Lu threw him a sharp glance. "He's married to your sister? So, how could you deny knowing him?"

Shrugging, Rui added: "Our family was large and a matchmaker found her a family to enter into as a child bride. I was only a child myself when she left the house and never saw her after she married." He shrugged again. "This is a common practice in my hometown."

Lu nodded and brought him back to his story. "So, what about Shih-hua?" he repeated.

"My sister carelessly told him about me one day. I don't know how she found out about me herself. Perhaps my mother still had some contact with her. I don't know. What I do know is that no one wants an ex-convict in the family, so her husband, Shih-hua, never told anyone. But he remembered," Rui added bitterly.

"You sold the bomb to Shih-hua," Lu stated.

"It's my bad fate." Rui exhaled loudly, dropped his shoulders, and hung his head.

Lu ordered Ma to bind Rui Ren's hands and Zhang to arrest Liu Shih-hua for his older brother's murder.

Once again in the yamen's office, Lu sat drinking tea with Fu-hao, Ma, and Zhang.

"How did you know Rui had been in the military?" Fu-hao asked.

"He said he was from Hunan but had lived in Shaanxi province. He's not a merchant. Therefore, what would take him to such a remote area? The Emperor has a large army stationed along the border to protect the country from the Mongols. Many of those soldiers are criminals serving out their sentences. It was a reasonable deduction." Lu took a sip of his tea.

"Ah," Ma said, "then the connection with the bomb became obvious." He smacked his lips.

Fu-hao's face tightened and he shot an irritated glance at Ma. Lu hid a grin. He knew his brother felt Ma and Zhang took too many liberties.

"But why did Shih-hua do it? Why kill his older brother?" Zhang asked.

"That's the saddest part of all. With their father retired, the older brother had all the power and authority of running the family and their business. Unfortunately, his drinking and carousing was destroying the family."

"Making killing Shih-kuei seem the only solution," Zhang said.

"But an older brother," Fu-hao lamented. "That's a crime against nature."

Lu glanced at his younger brother, his confidant and court secretary, and counted his blessings.

Originally published as "Fireworks, from Judge Lu's Ming Dynasty Case Files" in *Flash and Bang: A Short Mystery Fiction Society Anthology*, ed. J. Alan Hartman (Untreed Reads 2015) pages 19-30.

CHAPTER 6
PIGS AND BRIGANDS

"They beat me and knocked me down." The man's thin hands shook, although whether in anger or fear, Judge Lu couldn't say. The court's morning session began with this traveling merchant's case of highway robbery as he was coming to town late last night.

"When I fell, their leader laughed and pressed his foot on my neck. As I lay spread out on the ground, he threatened to kill me, taunting me, making me grovel like a dog," the complainant said, shaking even more.

"And then?" Lu encouraged him to continue.

"After stripping me down to my leggings, they bound me, knocked me unconscious, and left me there on the road." The more he talked, the more crimson his face became. He brushed a hand across his forehead.

"So, you say you were coming to town to sell a load of sorghum and they accosted you outside the city. How many were there? Do you think you could recognize the brigands?" Lu asked.

"There were at least four or more men, Your Honor!" the merchant said in a high-pitched voice. "They took everything. Everything. That sorghum would have fetched a good price. The grain was excellent and I already had a buyer. It would have made the best whiskey. I was counting on that money to see me through until next year. I am ruined. Ruined." He hung his head as if counting his losses.

"And the men? What did they look like?" The judge asked again in a firm, even tone. The merchant appeared to be in shock. Lu didn't want to push him too much more, but he needed a description for his soldiers to use when he sent them out to hunt for the criminals. Maintaining peace and preventing highway robbery were at the top of his list of responsibilities as Magistrate in the area.

"They were all big fellows. And mean," the merchant said.

Lu sighed. "Be more—"

"Your Honor, Your Honor, please excuse this interruption!" A taller, younger version of the judge had entered from the back of the court, behind the magistrate's desk. He moved quickly to Lu's side, keeping his head low. Urgency caused his words to run together.

Lu, surprised at this interruption by his brother and personal secretary, Lu Fu-hao, leaned toward him to catch every word.

"Chu Ming-yuan, the local security team leader, brought in a man accused of killing his neighbor."

Shaking his head, Lu frowned. What was happening to his province? Highway robbers, murderers? The Emperor will certainly think he's incapable. The weight of his formal gown with its large, square badge of office embroidered on front, pressed down on his shoulders; his black magistrate's hat, with its generous wings standing out on each side, sat uncomfortably on his head.

The judge looked over at his court recorder and said, "Secretary Lu Fu-hao will finish the interview with merchant Zhou."

To Fu-hao he said, "Take merchant Zhou to the office for the rest of his complaint, then return to court immediately.

"Ma, bring in the security team's leader," he ordered his personal guard, who stood nearby against the side wall.

In short order, a rotund, middle-aged man wearing leggings and a thigh-length coat stomped through the substantial double doors directly opposite Lu.

"Your Honor," he said, the note of pride unmistakable in his voice, "we have captured Farmer Song. He murdered his neighbor, Farmer Feng. Although Song tried to escape, we were able to seize him without loss to our team."

Judge Lu's eyes widened. He stared hard at Chu Ming-yuan. "Did you make a formal report to the court secretary?"

The man's shoulders dropped. "Not yet, Your Honor. I wanted to let you, as Father of this province, know as soon as possible. I will attend to the report immediately after leaving Your Honor's presence."

"See to it. A report must always be filed before seeking admittance to court." Lu rubbed his brow. Systems must be followed. Everything, including the initial formal report, had to be included in the case files. He scowled at the security team's leader. "I will excuse you this time, but follow the rules in the future.

"Is the body secure and left as you found it?" Lu asked.

Ducking his head at the reprimand, Chu said, "Feng's brother, Feng Da-jiao, demanded that he be allowed to move the body inside. He said leaving his brother on the ground showed disrespect to his spirit."

Lu frowned and glared at the security leader. "You know the law. I must view the site and the body. How dare you allow the body to be moved?" He was exasperated with the sloppiness he found in the province. To carry out justice, the law must be followed. Hiding his frustration, he thrust out his hand to indicate that he should proceed.

Chu continued in a subdued tone, "My men are holding the murderer, Farmer Song, outside the gate. At your command we will bring him before the court."

"Do so."

At that, Chu pressed his hands together in front of his chest and backed out of the court. Within minutes he appeared once again. This time he was accompanied by three men pulling a bound and scuffed-up man. Once in front of Lu, they pressed the prisoner to his knees and stood aside at attention.

"Your Honor, this man, known as Farmer Song, is accused of murdering his neighbor Farmer Feng."

"Why are you accusing Farmer Song of the murder? What evidence do you have against him? Has he confessed?"

Chu straightened his shoulders and held his head higher. "Feng Da-jiao found his brother, Farmer Feng, dead near his shed. He alerted us and accused Song of the murder."

"Did Da-jiao see Song murder his brother? Why is he accusing him?"

"Farmer Song has a long history of conflict with his neighbor. Song's boar has escaped many times and each time devastated Feng's garden. Yesterday, Song had a heated argument with Feng again. He pushed Feng and threatened him. Da-jiao had to intervene because Song had become violent."

"Where was this?"

"On the street in front of Feng's home."

"Did anyone else see this altercation?"

"Many people, Your Honor."

Judge Lu pointed at the man cringing on the floor in front of him. "Farmer Song, you stand accused of murdering your neighbor. Do you confess to the crime?" His voice boomed across the courtroom.

Song fell forward on his knees, beating his head on the floor. "Your Honor, I did not kill Feng!" His voice quivered.

"You two have a history of violent conflict, and you were heard threatening him the day he died. You might as well confess. We will get the truth from you, eventually." Lu looked meaningfully over at the jailer standing along the side wall. When criminals refused to confess to their crimes, the court had other, more concrete, ways of convincing the perpetrator to admit guilt.

Song followed his gaze and began hitting his head even harder on the floor. "Please, Your Honor! We argued, yes, but I never hurt him. He was alive when I left."

"Guards, take Song to jail. Hold him, but do not apply any torture until I give the order." Lu glared at the jailer. "I expect you to protect him while he's in your custody, understand?"

The jailer snapped to attention and bowed. Lu was only too aware of the jailer and his underlings demanding cash in return for either not using torture on the criminal or to use a lighter form of torture if the court required it.

"Chu, remain here and file a proper report for the court.

"Zhang, bring a contingent of soldiers over to Farmer Song's to protect his property from vandals and thieves." Lu added this precautionary measure to keep locals from looting and destroying the accused's property, as often happened. "After the soldiers are dispatched, return here immediately.

"Ma, I want you to investigate in the neighborhood. Find out everything you can about Feng and Song. There's a wine shop near the farms, start there.

"Fu-hao, bring your writing materials. We'll leave for the homicide site immediately."

Lu and his entourage arrived in front of a low-roofed, mud house with patches of stucco missing. Zhang pounded loudly on the simple, but strongly built, wood door. A short, muscular man opened it and stood staring at Zhang while scratching his head. The odor of garlic mixed with onion embraced Lu.

"Magistrate Lu is here to inspect the victim and the homicide site," Zhang announced.

The man jumped back a step and peered beyond Zhang, catching sight of Lu on his horse, dressed in his official magistrate robes. "Of course! I am honored, Your Honor," he said as, hands clasped at chest level, he bobbed up and down from his waist. "My brother is lying within. Please come."

Lu entered a dim room with one wooden table and a few stools placed near the earthen stove built into the side wall. Across from that lay the body of a man of medium build. As soon as Fu-hao set up his table and prepared his ink, Lu moved toward the body and bent over, inspecting it. The killing blow left a knife wound in the back and appeared to have been delivered with an upward thrust, indicating the killer might have been shorter than the victim.

"Knifed in the back. He probably didn't even know Song was attacking him," Da-jiao said as Lu stood up.

Lu nodded. "Take me to where you found him."

Da-jiao took Lu out to a small shed with an animal enclosure running down its side. They walked along the fence's edge to the far corner. "Here, he was lying near the pigpen's gate."

A sow covered in mud watched them from within the pen. A portion of her fence had been recently repaired.

"Is she the reason Farmer Song's boar comes over," Lu asked with a grin.

"Her, and the garden." Feng's brother stabbed a finger toward a small patch of barely visible disturbed ground on the other side of the shed and spat. "Stupid pig. He's totally destroyed it. Nothing but mud now."

"How about your brother's sow? Did she ever break out and destroy the garden? It looks like part of the fence has been repaired."

"She's a good old pig, stays put. She gets plenty of scraps. Just eats and sleeps. No, Song's boar broke through the fence. He's a terror. My brother was fed up and planned to sue for damages. That's what the fight was about. He told Song he was going to pay, and pay big, for what his boar had done." He swung around toward Lu. "We deserve justice."

"And you shall have it. However, it is critical for the court to follow procedures. In the end, justice will be served."

Lu proceeded to closely study the ground. Feng's brother walked to the shed and watched from a non-interfering distance. Fu-hao had moved his makeshift table and chair near Lu, ready to record the findings. The entire area was covered with the recent footprints of the curious and those who assisted in moving the body.

"Did anyone find a knife?" Lu called to Feng's brother.

"No. Nothing. Song must have taken it with him."

"It's impossible to delineate anything," Lu groused to Fu-hao. "Too many people have tramped through here. I need to remind the citizens not to disturb crime scenes. Hang a notice to that effect on the court's public entrance. Everyone coming to court should see it. Also, put the topic on the agenda for our community meeting this week." He turned away in disgust. "What a mess. Let's hope Ma was able to glean some useful information at the wine shop."

Feng's sow grunted.

"See, even the pig knows better," Lu said with a sardonic grin.

Late in the evening, Ma returned from the wine shop. He'd

abandoned his uniform, and wore a simple pair of trousers tied below the knee over leggings and a short jacket tied at the waist. Lu, wearing a casual long gray robe, sat at ease around a small tea table with Fu-hao and Zhang. They had been discussing the Feng murder case.

As his guard entered the office, noting Ma's bright red face, Lu said, "I hope you spent my money wisely." Whenever his guard drank, his face betrayed his indulgence. However, such a telltale sign never stopped his guard from enjoying a drink or two.

"Come, sit, have some tea, and tell us what you discovered." Lu said.

Ma bowed, folded his rangy frame on the chair, and joined the others.

"The wine shop turned out to be a true treasure," Ma began. "According to the men there, Feng Da-jiao, the victim's younger brother, is the leader of a local gang. They make a living shaking down travelers, and have even been known to rob traveling merchants."

Lu raised an eyebrow and nodded. "Very interesting. What else?"

"I discovered two, possibly related—or not related, things," Ma said and paused, his eyes seeming to travel to the ceiling.

Lu grimaced. His guard was fond of over-thinking information and creating complex scenarios where none existed.

"Ma..."

"Yes, Sir," he said as if awakened from a reverie. "The gossip is that Feng had a long-standing conflict with Song. The two are well-known for their heated, sometimes violent arguments. Always over that boar of Song's. Second, it is common knowledge that Feng liked to gamble, was heavily in debt, and was planning on selling his farm."

"Excellent. Excellent," Lu said. He studied the table's dark grain as he considered this new information.

"One more thing," Ma said.

"Yes?"

"There is another wine shop nearby, where Da-jiao and his men spend a lot of time. If you would like, I could go there tonight."

Lu continued to study the wood grain with its parallel lines meeting and eventually becoming one connected line. Finally, after a few seconds of silence, he leaned back in his chair. "We will go to Da-jiao's wine shop," he said.

Fu-hao cringed. "Don't do that. You're the magistrate. You'll be recognized. It's unbecoming. Such work should be—"

Lu flicked his palm towards his brother and stopped Fu-hao before he could complete his thought. "When I'm on duty, people recognize the power of my official uniform: the badge, black robe, and hat. That's really all they pay attention to, all they see. Don't worry, little brother, now they will see only a simple, scruffy worker."

Lu stood up, threw his robe down on the chair, and left the room to change his clothing. Ma and Zhang smiled broadly. This would be a fun night.

The stench of sweat, rancid cooking oil, and bad wine filled the room. Figures, barely illuminated by a grease-spotted, hanging lantern, sat hunched over tables. A hearty blanket of voices, punctuated now and then with laughter, spread over the drinkers.

When Ma, Zhang, and Lu entered the room, everyone fell silent while they studied the new arrivals. Lu slouched over and walked with a slight limp as he followed his two guards to a table in a corner. Little of the lantern light reached to their table. Lu sat in the deepest shadow, facing out into the room. Ma and Zhang sat on stools on either side of the judge, each turned at an angle facing into the room. They placed their order: a large jug of wine and a plate of onion cakes. The room remained silent.

After the wine and food arrived, a familiar short, burly fellow approached their table. Lu ducked his head and held his wine cup up, covering his lower face. Ma bent slightly forward, hiding the magistrate's figure even more.

"Welcome, strangers. What brings you here?" Da-jiao said.

Zhang rose up, "Ah, Master Feng Da-jiao! Come and join us."

Da-jiao started, clearly not expecting strangers to recognize him. "Who are you? How do you know me?"

Zhang laughed. "I'm a court guard under the new magistrate," Zhang said. "I was at your house today."

"Ah. Yes," Da-jiao said peering at Zhang as if trying to place him. Seldom are servants remarkable enough to be remembered. "And you two?" he said turning to Ma and Lu.

Ma leaned forward in greeting. Lu, wearing a stained shirt and worker's hat tied around his head, slouched over the table but managed to remain in the darkest shadows.

"We're also with the new administration," Ma said. "We needed a drink and heard this was *the place to come*," he added, dropping his tone to emphasize a meaning beyond the words.

Da-jiao's half smile indicated that he knew what Ma meant. He pulled up a stool and sat down. "Yes, if you're looking for 'extra income' this is the place. If you can do the work."

"No problem there," Ma said as he raised a hand to let the watchful owner know they needed another wine cup for Da-jiao.

After the cup was placed on the table, Ma said, "But we must be with a gang that knows what's what. We heard this was the place to link up with such a group. Rumor has it you all have had a profitable year." He filled the extra wine cup and, holding it in two hands, offered it to the gang leader.

Da-jiao grinned, took the cup, and emptied it in one swig. "A profitable year and a profitable week! We are in the middle of a very *profitable* exchange from a recent job," he said.

Ma refilled his cup and leaned toward him. "Could you use extra hands? My comrades," and he indicated Zhang and Lu, "are experienced."

"Would you put your court jobs at risk for such work?" Da-jiao asked, emptying his cup.

"Have you any idea what kind of pay we get for being on call day and night?" Ma returned. "If we don't supplement our pay, how can we survive? We couldn't even buy bad wine."

Da-jiao pushed back on the stool; guffawing loudly, he slapped the table. His laughter released the silence in the room and voices once more rose to fill the former void.

"It's possible we could use three good men, such as you." Da-jiao grabbed his cup and downed the wine in one gulp.

As soon as he slapped it back onto the table, Ma filled it again and raised his own cup, as if to drink. Da-jiao followed suit. Each time the gang leader emptied his cup, Ma refilled it.

"We know we're good, but what about you? We heard you and your gang are the best in this part of the province, but how do we know? We're risking everything if we work with you," Ma said.

Da-jiao spat on the floor and rubbed his chin. "Since your connections to court can be useful to me and my gang—not only in our normal activities, but also if we get into trouble with the law—I'll prove to you how successful we are. We just completed a job that's worth a lot of money. Tonight, we will move the goods over to our buyer. I'll take a chance with you three and let you work with us. Then you'll see." At this boast he again drained his cup.

"If you have so much that it needs several men to move it, where could you possibly hide it? The new magistrate is no fool. How can you hide so much without someone knowing?" Ma asked.

Da-jiao laughed. "I have the perfect place where no one would even think of looking. Today the magistrate was within a few feet of our treasure and he never even suspected."

At Ma and Zhang's skeptical glances, he added, "It's in my brother's shed, right next to the pigpen." His grating laughter rang throughout the room. Then, he abruptly stopped and said, "We must move the goods tonight and I am short a couple of men. If you'd like to join us, you can."

Ma jumped in, "We would be honored to join you and your gang tonight. Unfortunately, we have to attend to court business before the next sounding from the drum tower. When are you going to move the goods?"

"Waiting until after the drums sound will work, since it will be late and everyone will be asleep. After you have attended to your duties, come to my brother's."

The three rose from the table with Lu ducking his head and keeping in the shadows.

"We'll be there," Ma said. After a quick bow to Da-jiao, they left the wine shop.

Without a word, they strode back to the yamen. Once inside the gate, they moved along the shadowed wall, passing though the courtroom and then entering Lu's office.

"Zhang, dispatch another contingent of soldiers around Feng's home. Tell them to surreptitiously circle Feng's property, being as discrete as possible. When Da-jiao and his men arrive to retrieve the stolen merchandise, we'll arrest them."

At the drum tower's sounding the hour, Lu, Ma, and

Zhang left the yamen, rapidly moving through the sleeping city. As they approached the street to Feng's house, Ma moved to the front of the trio and Lu fell back.

Cumulus clouds lazily crossed the moon, further darkening the area. A nearby dog started barking, followed by a deep voice calling out for it to be quiet. Feng's house and yard came into sight and appeared to be empty.

"Over here. Around the back," a low voice directed.

The three swiveled toward the voice. A man's form stepped out from the inky blackness of the house's shadow. Da-jiao.

"You're in time to help move the sacks," he said. "We'll put them in the carts my men brought."

"Where do they go from here?" Ma asked as they rounded the house, sauntering toward the shed. Feng's sow lay in the same far corner she'd been in earlier, keeping an eye on the commotion.

"We'll take them to a whisky manufacturer fifteen *li* from here. He's paying a good price because the grain is such high quality." Lu could see Da-jiao's teeth as he grinned at Ma.

"So, it's sorghum. That comes from the north. How did you manage to get it?" Ma asked.

"You are awfully nosy, aren't you?" He lifted his chin in a prideful gesture. "Well, I'll tell you: a generous traveling merchant gave it to us." Da-jiao's laugh ended in a snort. He spat, then added, "Don't worry about him. He won't be bothering us; I took care of that."

Ma stood with his hands on his hips, looking at the shed. "This is a brilliant hiding place. Your brother's pig shed. Did he know you were using it?"

Da-jiao cast a long look at Ma. "You're no end of questions! What do you care? It's here and it's safe." He paused, then said, "It's not my brother's shed anymore. Now that he's dead, it's mine." He grinned. "Convenient timing, don't you think? Of course, I helped it along with that accursed Farmer Song."

"Ah, yes. Song killed your brother. Is that what you mean?" Ma said.

"Don't be stupid. Song is a weakling. He'd never be able to kill anyone. I'm amazed he can kill his chickens to eat." Da-jiao's contempt for the young farmer was obvious.

Ma pushed on. "If he didn't kill your brother, who did?"

"You can work that one out for yourself. Now, let's get moving," Da-jiao said.

He strode to the shed and stopped. The door was ajar. A snuffling-like noise came from inside. Da-jiao held his hand up, halting his men, and guardedly moved forward. When he was within an arm's distance from the door, he swung his hand around, indicating he wanted his men to line up on either side of the door. Lu, Ma, and Zhang went to the darker side behind the shed's door; the others went to its open side.

With one rapid thrust, Da-jiao pushed the door completely open. "Come out of there, you turtle's egg!"

The noise stopped. No one moved.

"I said, come out. Now. If you value your life."

Silence.

Da-jiao ordered one of his men to light a lantern. Lu moved further into the door's shadow and behind Zhang. Ma stepped forward into the flickering light.

As Da-jiao plunged the lighted lantern into the shed, he called out, "Aargh! It's that blasted boar! He's gotten into the sacks and there's grain everywhere. I'm going to kill him!"

Before Da-jiao could grab his knife, Lu called out, "You're all under arrest by order of the court!"

Da-jiao charged out of the shed as his men sprinted away. Ma grabbed for him. He swung his arm wide, pushing Ma aside. Zhang jumped out from behind, knocking Da-jiao down and pinning him to the ground. Lu called for his soldiers. They swarmed around, capturing the other bandits.

Judge Lu stared at the disheveled, badly bruised, man kneeling before him. Da-jiao's heavily sweat-stained and torn clothing, along with his glazed eyes and sloping posture, told Lu much about his time in the hands of the court's jailer. Gone was his sauntering arrogance, replaced by defeat, if not contrition.

Lu had the courtroom doors opened, allowing the citizens to view the trial. After filling the allowable space, the over-flow of observers stood outside the massive doors. They waited. Only the swishing of soft-soled shoes on the stone floor betrayed their presence.

"Feng Da-jiao, you stand accused of multiple crimes: robbing and beating merchant Zhou; falsely accusing Farmer Song of murder; and committing the most heinous crime of murdering an elder brother. Do you confess to each of these crimes?" Lu intoned.

"I do, Your Honor," Da-jiao replied in a barely audible voice.

With those words two major cases—one involving highway robbery and the other murder—were closed. Lu breathed in deeply. Justice had been served once more. He had fulfilled his duties to the emperor and to the people.

Originally published as "Double Trouble, from Judge Lu's Ming Dynasty Case Files," in the online magazine Kings River Life (July 12, 2015): *http://kingsriverlife.com/08/29/double-trouble-from-judge-lus-ming-dynasty-case-files/*.

CHAPTER 7
THE PEDDLER

The cheerful tinkling of small bells contrasted starkly with the muted, bloodied body at Judge Lu's feet. He glanced over his shoulder and toward the bells' source. A small crowd of curious onlookers had formed nearby.

A tall man wore a soft, dark hat tied with a red ribbon; a broken mugwort sprig projected out above his ear. Clearly, he was a peddler. Two containers, covered with candy-colored scenes from stories past, sat on the ground near him. An umbrella projected out of one of them. Bells hung among talismans with good-luck sayings, swinging in the moist breeze atop a green and blue umbrella. The whole display was designed to draw the eyes of passersby and entice them to buy a trinket. Now, the carefully constructed cheerfulness went unnoticed.

Ma, Lu's personal guard, kept the spectators at bay, allowing the judge to focus on his own, more gruesome, duties. Lu turned back to the victim and his task of examining the crime scene. Distance from the viewers and the early morning mist gave the dead man privacy. It was the least they could do for him, no matter who he was.

Lu knew his guard wasn't the only reason the crowd had yet to push its way inside. Certainly, the man's brutal and untimely death had left his spirit angry. No one wanted to risk inciting the ghost's wrath and possible repercussions by getting involved. Intrigue held the curious, but fear kept them standing apart as silent observers.

Fu-hao, Lu's court secretary and younger brother, cleared his throat and rustled the papers he had on the make-shift table in front of him. Lu turned back to the corpse and his job.

"The victim is lying face down in the dirt, as if hit from behind," Lu worked to keep his voice neutral as he reported his findings so that Fu-hao could take notes. He reached out and removed a soft, dark cotton hat from the man's head. Steeling himself, he pushed his fingers through thick, matted hair. "The back of the victim's skull has broken bones. The depression is straight, not round." Precision in observation was not a choice; it was essential.

He stood up and flicked his hand twice to tell Zhang, his second personal guard, to turn the body over. Then he leaned forward and opened the man's shirt. No marks. He flicked his hand again. Zhang rolled the body over, exposing the now bare back. No marks.

"I do not see any other signs of trauma. It appears that someone hit the man from behind with one strong blow, which killed him. Death is due to unnatural causes. He was murdered."

A gasp went up from the crowd. Lu ignored them. Leaving the corpse's face and body exposed, he slowly moved away.

Nearby, still attached to a bamboo carrying pole, but sitting at odd angles, were two baskets of breakfast dumplings. They had tumbled indiscriminately out onto the ground, their once smooth, creamy-colored surfaces now speckled with dirt. Lu systematically circled the body, picking up a few items which appeared out of place: bird feathers, a short stem with mugwort leaves, a dirty piece of cloth, and a straight, flexible wire about three hands in length. With his back to the crowd, he tucked each one unobtrusively into his gray coat's wide sleeves.

Stepping near the body once more, he signaled Zhang to cover it and dispatched another of his soldiers to find out what was keeping his coroner. The coroner's job was more of a political appointment than a medical specialist's position, so Lu didn't expect much from his examination. In any case, the law required he examine the body himself rather than rely solely on secondary information.

The crowd had grown. There were now a few peddlers with their various wares along with the collection of random citizens. Two more of the peddlers drew Lu's attention.

One, a short, portly man with a round face, appeared either concerned or curious. Lu couldn't quite decide. His wares of a dozen or so round drums, clappers, small cymbals, and other percussion instruments of various sizes hung off a strap that ran around his neck. The multicolored strip tying his cloth hat in place sported a tiny toy double drum. The back of his right hand pressed against his forehead as he held two long, narrow wooden clappers to shadow his eyes. His left hand hung at his side, enclosing several long, thin metal mallets.

Next to the drum peddler stood an elderly man with an over-flowing cart. Long, narrow bands of paper fluttered above layers of stacked song-bird cages from the cart's protective, red and blue cloth roof. He also wore the typical merchant's clothing of a short coat over leggings and a muted crumpled hat held in place by a strip of red cloth. A spray of white blossoms tucked behind his ear gave him a friendly "trust-me" appearance and bobbed as he gently caressed a white bird nestled in his hand.

Judge Lu stroked his left sleeve, a frown on his face. Had he picked up clues to the murderer or simply items lost beforehand? These peddlers probably came daily to sell their wares. He walked over to the impromptu investigative area set up for him and his entourage and sat in a folding chair near Fu-hao. This inquisition wouldn't have the formal and imposing trappings of the official court—neither the setting nor his own official robes—but he wanted to get as much information as possible while details were still fresh in people's minds.

"Bring those three merchants over," he ordered Zhang, pointing out the peddlers.

Surreptitiously observing the men, he saw them blanch. Good. That was the reaction he was hoping to get. The only thing worse than fear of ghosts was fear of the government and its courts.

Once Zhang had rounded up the peddlers, Lu directed them to come forward. They all approached with alacrity and immediately fell to their knees before him. He silently scrutinized their bent forms.

"Tell me what you know of this man," Lu ordered. He allowed a cold, hard edge to mold his voice.

The tall peddler spoke up. "He's a stranger. I come here regularly. My spot is at the front of the path. He's not from here."

The bird peddler shook his head. "He's a peddler, that's for sure, but I have never seen him before."

"And what do you say?" Lu asked the rotund drum peddler.

The squat peddler seemed to shrink from the first man. "I don't know. I can't be sure. I have my own business and no time for being nosy."

"I'm sure that's true. But you did recognize him, didn't you?"

The man ducked his head.

"Don't hide the truth. Tell the court."

Exhaling as if defeated, he said, "Yes. He has been around the past couple of days. He sold dumplings, but he wanted a site to expand his business. Even though times are hard and fewer people have money to buy, this park gets a lot of traffic and so he wanted to establish a spot."

The first peddler's face twisted and he was about to spit, but after a quick glance at Zhang, he swallowed hard instead.

"Did he find a spot?" Lu asked.

The drum peddler shrugged, turned his head away from the body, and murmured, "I don't think so."

Lu leaned forward. "Why not? All he needed was a patch of ground." He waved a hand out toward the park's grounds. "There's plenty of space for another peddler."

Before the drum peddler had a chance to respond, the first peddler said, "Nonsense. I'm at the entrance gate. If he'd been here before, don't you think I'd notice?"

The drum peddler glared. "Are you questioning my honesty? Why would I make that up?"

"How would I know why you'd do it? Maybe you're trying to throw the blame on someone else. Maybe you killed him, hitting him with one of your mallets."

The drum peddler jerked backwards and began to rise up. Zhang laid a massive hand on his shoulder, pushing him back down.

Judge Lu hid his annoyance. The men were getting out of hand. Here in the park, without the formal court's ambience, they were forgetting how critical their words and demeanor were. He glanced at Fu-hao, who was writing quickly, taking everything down for the court record.

"Tell the court about seeing this man earlier," Lu said to the drum peddler.

"I didn't talk to him. But, I'd say that he'd been starting to sell his dumplings already over the past two days. He carried them in baskets on his pole, but he seemed to stay mostly in one spot. I don't think he moved around much. I'd guess he was looking to set up a regular location. We all do. People get to know where you are and where to come for a special treat or to buy gifts."

"Where are you set up?"

"On the other side of that bamboo." He pointed to a small clump of bamboo slightly down and on the other side of the dirt path in front of them.

"How could you see him from your stand if you were on the other side of the bamboo?" Lu asked.

The peddler rubbed his right leg. "I have trouble standing all day and frequently sit on a stool near my drums. From such a low position, I can see down the lane pretty well."

At that, the elderly bird peddler chimed in. "Yesterday, a screaming child scared my favorite bird and it flew into those bushes," he gestured toward a stand of low, green bushes nearby. "I had to come over and coax her back. I'm sure if this fellow had been at the front gate I would have noticed him."

Lu nodded and turned to the first peddler.

"You also deny seeing this man. According to your friend here," Judge Lu pointed to the drum peddler, "he'd have been close to you and your makeshift stand."

"I don't know what that fool is talking about. He must have seen someone else. There are lots of peddlers in the park, and the ones carrying baskets all look pretty much the same from a distance. That spot up front is mine and no one else was there, I can tell you that."

Judge Lu stroked his chin and tugged at his ear. He gazed at the three before him. They all sold their wares in the same area. Why would one claim to have seen the dead man and the others not? He remained silently contemplating the men a moment longer, then leaned back into his chair.

"Tell me about your local peddler's guild," he said to the drum peddler.

Lu thought an almost imperceptible grimace flashed across his face before he answered.

"It's true that a peddler's guild is being set up. At this point, not everyone belongs to it. There are many questions needing to be considered."

"Who is its leader?"

The drum peddler cast a quick glance to his left. The elder peddler spoke up. "I am the leader. There is a need to organize the peddlers so that we are not working against each other. If we don't, how can any of us succeed in these difficult economic times? As a group we can protect our own."

Lu turned toward the first man. "And you also belong to this guild?"

"He does," the elder peddler answered for him. "My nephew here has been essential in helping to convince the others to join together with us."

"So, if the dumpling seller wanted to remain here, he would have joined your group?"

"The organization would decide if he could join or not," the elder said.

"Why do you think this drum peddler insists that he saw the man for the past couple of days, when he obviously wasn't here?" Lu asked in a friendly voice as he tapped his chin.

The elder shook his head. "I can only assume that he is lying. He killed the man himself and he's trying to throw the court off, by opening up a world of other people to investigate in the death."

"That's not so!" The drum peddler jumped up; however, before he could say anything else, Zhang had thrown him back down into a kneeling position, his hand holding him in place.

"I didn't do it. He did." Shaking, he pointed a finger at the first peddler.

The man laughed scornfully. "No. You did and you'll pay for it."

The drum peddler banged his head on the ground before the judge. "Please, Your Honor, I can prove I'm not guilty."

"Then do so immediately or you're going to jail."

"Look in the container with the umbrella. You'll find the murder weapon there."

"Zhang, open the container," Lu ordered.

The first peddler's face lost all color as he watched the guard step over to his candy-colored containers still held together on his bamboo carrying pole.

Zhang pulled open a door on the side of his largest container and extracted a sturdy rod. He handed it to the judge, who examined it. A dark, tacky substance covered much of it. Blood. He held it up, and the first peddler groaned as he collapsed onto the ground.

———

Back in his office, Fu-hao finished the official report for Judge Lu's superiors. Setting his brush aside, he asked his brother what made him think the two were working together against the one, instead of the other way around. And why he asked about the peddler's guild.

"It is to be expected that the peddlers would want to organize and, as is common, often the members are related in one way or another."

"But then, why did they turn on the drum peddler? As a guild, they should have protected him and he should have protected them." Fu-hao shook his head in confusion.

"Remember, the drum peddler said that not everyone belonged to the guild. I noticed that both the first and elder merchant wore red bands around their hats; such a device is not uncommon for indicating membership in a group. The drum peddler wore a multicolored band. He was not a member of the guild."

"But why kill the dumpling peddler? What does the guild have to do with that?"

"The drum peddler has been selling in the park for years; he had a right to be there. In time, the guild would have persuaded him to join. But the dumpling peddler was different. By setting up his business in the park, and even in its best spot, the newcomer was breaking the guild's unspoken rules. He was aggressively going after the few coins people had to spend and was, therefore, a threat to the other peddlers' livelihoods and survival. It's a classic example of *fēn dào yáng biāo*—of people going their separate ways, without regard for others."

Fu-hao shook his head as he gathered the finished report's papers together. Tomorrow, the case would be sent to Judge Lu's superiors for review and confirmation of Lu's verdict of guilt.

Originally published as "The Peddler, from Judge Lu's Ming Dynasty Case Files" in *Elements in Writing: Anthology #9*, ed. Bradley D. Watson. (Saturday Writers 2016), pages 359-368.

CHAPTER 8
THE MISSING CONCUBINE

Judge Lu sensed his personal guards, Zhang and Ma, hovering at his door. Ignoring them, he continued to bury his head in a pile of case reports requiring his attention. He'd been out of town for a couple of days and needed to catch up. By law, cases were time-limited and had to be solved quickly and efficiently. Eventually, his guards' palpable tension forced him to look up.

As if taking that as a sign to approach, they marched into the office, their faces projecting excitement.

"What is it?" Lu asked.

"Sir, we've news about pharmacist Master Ying's second wife's death, the one your coroner determined died from unnatural causes," Ma said.

Lu pulled up the last case on his desk. It was Master Ying's official accusation against his concubine. In the document, Ying alleged his concubine killed his second wife, stole her jewels, and fled. The coroner's report, saying the wife had died of poisoning, was attached.

Glancing up from the document, Lu said, "This looks like

a straightforward case of murder and theft. Has the concubine been caught?"

"No Sir, not yet. Regarding this household, you might be interested in knowing that Zhang and I just came from a wine shop near the Ying compound. The gossip is that Master Ying's clerk, Cao, was having an affair with Master Ying's first wife," Ma said.

The judge drew his eyebrows together in disapproval.

"Adultery is a crime with a punishment of one hundred strokes with a heavy stick; however, the court won't get involved unless the husband makes a complaint," Lu said. He shook his head at Master Ying's bad fortune.

"People heard Clerk Cao claim that if Ying's wife were free, she'd be his," Ma added. "They think he attempted to murder Ying and killed the second wife by mistake."

"I talked with Old Woman Han, who shops for the Ying women," Zhang broke in. "She claims the husband was bad tempered and violent. His wives and concubine frequently had unusual bruises."

"Indeed. Well, according to the coroner," Lu again paged through the report, "except for interviewing Ying, none of the household family or staff were questioned. That was an opportunity lost." While a makeshift inquiry could be set up at the scene of a crime, further inquiries occurred in court, in public. He pressed his lips into a frown. "We need to find out what the staff in the Ying women's quarters know. I don't want to bring the women into court for questioning. It's too embarrassing for Master Ying to have his women paraded before everyone."

"We could hide in the women's quarters and eavesdrop," Zhang volunteered a bit too enthusiastically.

Lu shot him a cold look. "There will be no need." Having a strange male breaching all semblance of propriety, even for an official investigation, would humiliate both the court and the Ying family.

Undeterred, Zhang piped up again. "Right. We're soldiers and shouldn't be there. But you're the magistrate, you could—"

Ma punched him on the shoulder. "How dare you suggest Judge Lu do such a thing! Have you no sense at all? It would ruin him if he was found in the women's quarters. His career would be over!"

Lu nodded. The wheels of justice were already turning; all he had to do was let them move ahead. Once the concubine was arrested and convicted, Master Ying and the law would be satisfied. Case closed. He wouldn't have to look any further and expose Ying's other family problems.

Yet, given his guards' information, that scenario posed at least three problems. First, there would be a miscarriage of justice if the court found an innocent woman guilty of murder and executed her. Second, if the concubine was innocent, a murderer remained on the loose. Third, if the clerk and the first wife were guilty, Master Ying's life remained in danger and his death would be on Lu's hands.

On the other hand, if the concubine was, in fact, guilty, Master Ying would be furious at the loss of face he would suffer if the investigation went forward and displayed his dirty laundry for the world to see: his wife's infidelity, his own uncontrolled violence. Ying would certainly try to make Judge Lu suffer equally.

After a long silence, Lu said, "Bring in Old Woman Han. I want to talk to her."

The fear in the old marketer was obvious.

"Old Han," he said, using an address reflecting respect for

her age, "I understand you are known to the Ying household and do errands for the women of the family."

"Indeed, Sir. I have served the Ying household for more than ten years. I have always been honest and fair in my dealings." She grasped her hands firmly against her stomach as if protecting herself; however, her eyes were bright and direct.

"Of course. I've no doubt." He picked up a paper from his desk. "You've probably heard of Master Ying's second wife's death."

She sucked in a breath. "I know nothing about it. I was not at the house."

Studying her stiff, defensive posture, Lu suspected she was hiding how much she knew. She was, after all, a well-seasoned gossip. She had to be. Gossip was her stock in trade, useful in cementing relationships with the isolated elite women she visited.

He decided to take a non-confrontational approach, trusting that it would elicit more information. "No one suggested you were. Master Ying filed an accusation with the court and we need more information, which I hope to get with your assistance."

Old Han watched his face expectantly, but cautiously.

"I want you to go to the household and talk to the maids working in the women's quarters. Get them to tell you whatever they know or suspect about the death."

The woman readily agreed. "I always spend time with the maid servants, as well as their mistresses. It is not that they gossip. No, no. It's just that they are able to provide useful information for fulfilling the tasks their mistresses give me."

"Just so." He paused. "I would also like you to open the back gate leading onto the street. I will be there, waiting. You will let me inside."

Her eyes opened wide in surprise and she nervously glanced around the room, as if trying to discover if this was a trap. Lu understood her increasing panic. Women in her position were often accused of abetting illegal love affairs. If found out, they could be charged with a crime and severely beaten, which could lead to death.

"I assure you, my request is strictly in the pursuit of justice. Justice for both the murder victim and the accused."

He held her gaze. "It is imperative no one know I am there. Are you willing to help?"

Without further hesitation, Old Han agreed. "I'll go just before lunch to see Mistress Ying. Then, when she has lunch and her maids are waiting on her, I'll go to the servants' room. This would be the best time for me to let you into the compound. She likes to rest immediately after eating, and her maids have a chance to eat. That's when I'll ask your questions."

Lu, pleased at her quick-wittedness, grinned and began instructing her on his questions. While she kept a neutral demeanor, the gleam in her eyes betrayed her delight. For his part, Lu hoped his scheme wouldn't be discovered and lead to the demise of them all.

Before leaving the yamen, Lu changed from his formal robe into a short worker's jacket. He rolled his pant legs up and slipped on a pair of sandals. He told Zhang and Ma to do the same.

"Zhang, bring your Xiangqi game along," Lu said.

Zhang laughed, reached into his shirt, and displayed a folded piece of paper as well as a small sack of pebbles. "It's here, Sir. I never go far without it."

Xiangqi was a popular board game where three armies, representing the Three Kingdoms, battled against each other in order to capture their enemies' generals and take over their army.

Lu nodded, cast a discerning eye over his men, and directed them to follow. They went out through the back of the yamen to avoid inquisitive eyes.

Nearing the rear of the Ying compound, Lu split from his guards. The two walked along the opposite side from the walled mansion and settled down on their haunches across from its gate. To draw attention to themselves, they talked loudly, each baiting the other. Soon, leaving Zhang squatting over the board game spread out on the ground, Ma strode across the street.

"Friend, come play Xiangqi with us. We need a third," he called to the portly fellow guarding the Ying's back gate.

The fellow looked up and shook his head. "Can't. Have a job here. Can't leave."

"You won't be leaving. You'll be right across the street," Ma said. "We've got a bet on this game. You've got to come and help out." He looked up and down the street. "Nothing's happening. You can watch from there."

"Bring the game over and I can play here," the gatekeeper said.

Ma glanced over his shoulder. "He's already got it set up. Come on. What do you think is going to happen? Someone's going to steal the gate?" He laughed raucously.

"Well," the man glanced at the gate and then over at Zhang, "I guess it would be all right."

Ma made sure to sit across from Zhang, forcing the gate-keeper to drop onto his heels with his back to the Ying compound. Lu, standing at the end of the walled area, waited until the game had begun, then slowly made his way down the street. Once at the gate, he stopped and fiddled with his sandal. Soon the door fell ajar and he slipped through.

Old Woman Han chuckled when she saw his clothing. As

soon as he entered and the gate was relocked, she moved rapidly through a passageway along the outer wall, then turned into another passage. Lu hurried to keep up. After a couple more turns, she stopped, pointing to a recessed doorway and a nearby paper-covered latticed window.

Lu understood: from here he could hear the conversations between Old Han and the servants. When he nodded, she scurried down to the end of the building, turned, and vanished.

Lu stared along the now empty passage. He brushed the sweat from his forehead and inhaled deeply, taking in a lungful of spicy air. Tears sprang into his eyes as he fought to avoid coughing.

Cursing himself, he wondered what had gotten into him to try this stunt. Such hooliganism was more like something his impetuous younger brother would do. He stared down at his rumpled worker's clothing. If discovered, he'd be lucky if this was his future attire.

A noise from within—soft, shuffling sounds mixed with low, indistinct female voices—made him stiffen. He carefully checked the passage, then stepped nearer the window.

"Ah, Auntie, you've come to visit," a high-pitched, melodious voice called out. Old Han was known by "Auntie" to many, since it was at once a familiar and a respectful term.

Instantly, several voices called out greetings. Soon, the women settled down near the window for lunch.

"Such sadness in the household," Old Han said, clucking her tongue.

As if they had been waiting for someone to pour out their stories to, the women readily opened up to her.

"She was poisoned," one said.

"The Master said the poison was meant for him, but I don't think so," another said.

"Although there would be ample reason for it to be," came

another.

An uneasy silence followed this remark.

"Some people are saying Ying's concubine did it," Han said.

"What proof do they have?"

"People say she stole jewels and ran away. That's proof enough," Han said.

"Jasmine, tell her what you saw," a high-pitched voice ordered.

Haltingly, a timid voice said, "That day, before we found the young Mistress dead, Master Ying took a bundle into his shop at the front of the compound."

"That bundle was the so-called stolen jewels," the high-pitched voice asserted.

"Orchid, I understand you all might have bad feelings toward Master Ying, considering how he treats you, but really, why would he take jewels from his own house?" Old Han asked.

"He poisoned his wife and took her jewels to make his concubine look guilty," one of the women said.

"When his concubine first came here, she was not happy, but not unhappy, either. Within a few months, however, she seemed depressed, even miserable," Orchid said.

"Yes, yes. I met her. A charming woman," Han said, her voice sympathetic. "Too bad she was sold to Master Ying. That's her karma, though, and we all know we can't change fate. It doesn't make Master Ying guilty of falsely accusing her for his wife's murder. Anything could have been in that bundle. Besides, why would he take it to his store? He'd hide it someplace off his own property."

Lu couldn't help but smile. Picking Old Han to help him had been a good move. In spite of being illiterate, she could be an investigator herself. She knew how to follow up.

"Whatever he took was wrapped in a green and white

cloth. The Mistress's chrysanthemum embroidered green and white brocade shawl is missing. Plus, it was raining hard that day. All day. Water stood in the courtyard," Jasmine said.

"He hates being uncomfortable," Orchid offered. "He took it to his store because it was convenient. He walked along the veranda from our living area to his shop. There was no need for him to get wet."

"But why? Why blame his concubine for his wife's death? Not to mention, that would mean he knew his wife was poisoned," Old Han pushed.

Silence once more permeated the room.

Lu grinned again at the wily entrepreneur's questions.

"Are you saying he knew she was poisoned? That he did it?" Old Han asked.

"We can't accuse our Master," Orchid responded. "That is up to the judge. We know he's already tired of his concubine. He's constantly complaining about her weeping—which only causes him to beat her more. He often says he's wasted good money buying her, that he'd been better off buying a new sow for his farm."

"'Course, he also told his second wife she was a stone around his neck, just another mouth to feed," another added.

"If what you say is true, the magistrate needs to know," Old Han said.

"No one asked us," several women said in unison.

Lu shook his head; he should have been here to investigate the death himself.

"I've also heard the first wife may be involved somehow," Old Han led.

"Ah. Her unfortunate friendship," Orchid said. She sounded more sad than judgmental. Lu was surprised.

"Unfortunate friendship? What does that mean? She never leaves the house. Who could she have such a friendship with?"

"She doesn't have to go out of the compound," Orchid said.

Then Old Han said, as if she just thought of it, "Ah, she's having an affair with someone who's managed to steal into the household. Could it be with Ying's clerk?"

A general murmur of dissent followed her question.

"She wasn't having an affair. Clerk Cao does manage to have an excuse to come and talk to her at least once a week. But only to talk," Orchid said.

"Maybe he'd like to have an affair," another said, "but she wouldn't. Never."

"Yet, Master Ying is not easy on her, either," Old Han mused.

"That's true," Orchid said. "He's short tempered with all his women, but she struggles to please him. Clerk Cao is seeking water for his thirst, but he'll never get it."

"Do you think Cao knows Master Ying beats her?" Old Han asked.

"Everyone knows that," Orchid said. "It's not a secret that can be easily hidden in the compound."

Old Woman Han asked a few more questions, but the responses were unenlightening, and so she left.

Lu stepped back into the doorway's shadow and waited.

"Sir, follow me," a voice whispered.

He wordlessly followed. The household was at rest; nevertheless, Han again rapidly walked ahead of him, checking at each break in the buildings. When they reached the rear exterior gate, Han unlatched the lock and Lu slipped through. He heard the lock fall into place as he paused to glance over at the gatekeeper still embroiled in the Xiangqi game.

As soon as Ma saw Lu, he yawned and stretched broadly. In doing so, he shoved against the paper board with his shoe. The game pieces went skittering in all directions. Zhang and the gatekeeper yelled and cursed at the ruins.

Lu ambled to the corner and waited. What he'd overheard was worth the unconventional means he'd used. Especially since he didn't get caught. Now he had a clear idea of how to proceed.

"Before we return to the yamen," Lu said when his men joined him, "I must stop at Ying's pharmacy and check for the stolen jewels."

"Like that, Sir?" Zhang asked, eyeing his costume.

Lu looked down at his worker's outfit. "Hmm. No. We'll return to the office and you two will come back with an official order to search the shop. Then you will return to court with Clerk Cao."

They moved along at an easy pace and Lu filled them in on what he had overheard. He concluded by remarking that the women all appeared to think the concubine was innocent and Ying had poisoned his own wife and then blamed the concubine.

"If you don't mind my saying, Sir," Ma said, "they're women."

"Point being?" Lu asked.

"They like the concubine. At the same time, they hate their Master because he isn't easy to work for. They're being emotional. Besides, it's just gossip. None of them spoke up when the coroner was at the house."

"Yes," Zhang said, not to be outdone by Ma. "As for the concubine, women often commit suicide to escape misery. Murder is a man's game. I still think Clerk Cao did it. Passion could drive him to murder."

"Cao definitely has motivation," Lu said. "He could have believed he was protecting his love, the first wife, or he could think that once she is widowed, she would be open to marrying him. In that case, instead of murdering the husband, through bad karma, the second wife may have accidently taken the poison, which killed her. For all these reasons, we must search the shop for the jewels and then I must question Clerk Cao at court."

———

Back at the yamen, Lu tried to review more reports; however, he found it impossible to focus. He kept listening for his men's return.

Finally, he heard boots hurrying toward his office. Ma appeared in the doorway carrying a bundle wrapped in a green brocade embroidered with white chrysanthemums. He placed it on Lu's desk. "I also brought the clerk back with me," he said. "Zhang is still at the store finishing our search. As soon as we found this, however, we thought you'd want to see it."

Lu nodded. "Good work." He unrolled the covering until a tangled mass of jewels fell out.

"Where did you find it?" he asked.

"In the store's back room, where Master Ying keeps supplies and mixes medicines. I found it tucked behind a large jar."

"Was Clerk Cao with you?"

"He had just come into the room. He seemed surprised and said he didn't know where it came from."

"Hmm. He would say that." Lu picked up the jewels.

"He could have been plotting with the first wife after all, and they were going to use them to pay for their escape," Ma said.

"On the other hand, one of the maids said she'd seen Master Ying leave with a bundle just like this on the day of his wife's death." Lu dropped the jewels back onto the cloth. "We shall soon find out."

He slipped on his court robes and black gauze hat with its wings on either side and strode into court. He took his place on the dais and called, "Bring in Clerk Cao for questioning."

A murmur went up from the audience hovering near the public entrance. Even though no announcement had gone out, the town already knew of the inquest. As Lu observed the onlookers, they split, allowing a middle-aged man to move to the front. Lu recognized Master Ying.

Clerk Cao trembled uncontrollably when he was deposited in front of the judge.

"What is your relationship with Madam Ying?" Lu demanded.

"I have no relationship with her, Your Honor."

"Liar! Tell me the truth, or I'll have to use more severe methods to force you to tell the truth."

Cao blanched. "It's true, Honorable Sir. I do see her on occasion to discuss business matters."

"Business matters! Since when does the wife of a pharmacist need to be consulted on business matters?" Lu glared at him, then turned toward a soldier standing on the side of the court. "Bring the thumb screws."

Although thumb screws were considered the lowest form of customary government torture, its use could result in permanent mutilation. Cao fell to his knees.

"Sir, perhaps I am interested in her, but she never, ever tried to tempt me in any way and never led me on. She is completely innocent of any wrongdoing." He was almost weeping as he finished his stuttered statement.

"That doesn't mean you wouldn't poison her husband, to remove him from your lustful path."

"If I wanted to kill Master Ying with poison, I would do it when he's having lunch in the store, to be sure he would eat it and die." Then, as if realizing his words could be taken to mean he'd been plotting his employer's death, he immediately added, "Not that I would, Your Honor."

Lu abruptly changed topics. "What of the jewels we found in the shop?" As Lu asked this, he also surreptitiously watched Master Ying.

At the mention of finding the jewels, Ying lost all color. Licking his lips, he looked towards the door.

Clerk Cao beat his head on the floor. "Your Honor, I knew nothing before your guard found the jewels this afternoon."

Leaving the man kneeling on the floor, Lu called out, "Bring Master Ying before the court."

Ying started back, but couldn't move through the tightly packed crowd. A guard grabbed him and dragged him before Lu.

"Master Ying, can you identify this cloth?" Lu asked.

"It belonged to my wife. It's been missing since my concubine stole her jewels."

"This was found in your shop, hidden behind a pot. How do you explain that?"

"My concubine must have hidden it, intending to come back and get it later."

Judge Lu looked at him askance. "You're saying your concubine, who is known to your entire household, hid these in your store when she fled, and she actually intended to come back later to retrieve the package without anyone noticing?"

Ying stared at the floor.

"Answer me," Lu ordered.

"I don't know what she intended, Sir. She was not a very bright woman."

"Yet she was bright enough to know how to mix the appropriate ingredients together to make a poison to kill you?"

"It was not uncommon for her to assist me in my preparations."

"Clerk Cao, did Master Ying's concubine assist in preparing clients' medicines?" Lu asked.

"No, Sir. She swept the floors and cleaned the shop. She never touched the herbs."

Ying seemed to look into the middle distance, his face unreadable.

"I have a witness who saw you carry this bundle out of your residence and into your shop," Lu said to Ying.

"Impossible. I didn't even know it was in my shop. Someone is lying," Ying said, but his hands were trembling so much he crossed his arms and tucked his hands into his sleeves.

Disgusted with Ying's apparently persistent lying, Lu leaned forward to challenge his words. Before the judge could ask more questions, however, Ma stepped up to him and whispered in his ear. Without a word, Lu left the court.

Zhang was pacing in the office. When he saw the judge, he stopped. "I believe I found Ying's concubine," he said, his face grim. "I examined the large barrels he uses to steep herbs and found a young woman's body in one that was sealed closed. She hasn't been there long. Ying's apprentice identified her as the concubine."

Lu shook his head. The level of cruelty people were capable of never ceased to surprise him.

Back in court, he stared at Ying for a long moment, then: "We've found your concubine's body—in your store. Ying, the court is charging you with the murder of your second wife and concubine, who you killed to cover up the first death."

Ying slumped, his face a sickly gray as he mumbled, "It wasn't my fault. She wouldn't stop weeping."

. . .

Originally published as "The Missing Concubine, from Judge Lu's Ming Dynasty Case Files" in *Fish Out of Water: A Guppy Anthology*, ed. Ramona DeFelice Long (Wildside Press, 2017) pages 16-26.

CHAPTER 9
THE UNSEEN OPPONENT

It wasn't until later that Judge Lu realized he had witnessed a murder on the ball field.

The game of kick ball followed Master Wang's celebratory sixtieth birthday dinner. The wealthy patriarch of a notable merchant family in Lu's district favored the highly competitive sport and today's opposing teams were each led by one of Master Wang's two sons.

During the game's first half, Judge Lu had been captivated by Master Wang's concubine. Fu-hao, his younger brother and court secretary, hadn't failed to notice.

"She may be aggressive, but I'll bet Master Wang doesn't mind. I'd certainly be willing to bed her any day," Fu-hao said grinning.

"Who?" Lu said, raising his eyebrows in response to his brother's comments and smirk.

He bent closer to Lu's ear. "You don't have to pretend you can't see how striking she is. Any man would notice her."

"You're too much," Lu grumbled. "Always thinking about women."

"And you, not enough. Life is more than work."

It wasn't that Lu hadn't noticed her. After all, how could he not? She was the only woman on the field, attacking the ball, kicking it with a power he hadn't expected. While women had played the game for generations, since the beginning of the current Ming Dynasty, it had become more and more a men's only pastime. Scrutinizing the young woman more closely, he considered her attributes. She was athletic, and she didn't have the tiny lotus feet so prevalent among the Han women of her class. As an ethnic Mongolian, her feet remained unbound, thereby allowing her to participate in such games.

Nevertheless, Lu did think Master Wang's oldest son, Huai-liang, could have kept her from scoring points a couple of times. He shook his head. Did Huai-liang give way to her because she was a woman? It wasn't surprising the younger son's team was ahead.

During the time-out, Lu surveyed the guests. Except for the patriarch, he knew only his own brother and his coroner, a local healer. Lu's familiarity with Master Wang came through governmental meetings with city elders. He'd been invited for today's celebration, and had accepted because, as the district magistrate, such gatherings were a part of his social duties.

Lu tugged impatiently at his long, dark, semi-formal robe. He admitted being more at ease working than socializing. Plus, he reflected, there was much to do back at the office, and spending all day dining and watching a game meant a long night of work ahead.

Lu glanced at Fu-hao chatting amiably amongst a group of young men. His brother had natural social skills and moved easily among unlikely strangers.

"Are you enjoying the game?" the portly Master Wang asked, interrupting Lu's musings.

"Your sons are excellent players."

"I've been fortunate," Wang said, rubbing a hand over his belly. "And my oldest son's boy looks like he will be a good player, too." He nodded toward a youngster who was standing close to Huai-liang.

Just then, one of the players tossed the ball—a red leather encased animal bladder filled with air—toward the boy. He kicked it, keeping it up, never touching it with his hands or elbows.

"Indeed. You seem to have a family of team players," Lu said. "Even your concubine shows excellent skills."

Wang brightened. "When I took Xiao Tai-tai as mine, some said I was foolish. She's almost forty years younger. But why shouldn't I? Besides, she can run the household. My first wife is getting old and my younger son's mother, my second wife, died last year."

Soon, the game resumed, with each side vying to breach the other team's line of defense by hitting the ball through a net placed in the middle of the field and to the other side.

Qiu-lin, the younger son, fell as he surged toward the ball. Wang's concubine seized the ball, kept it in the air, and booted it through the net.

The audience cheered.

Lu leaned forward, his attention on Qiu-lin, who now lay sprawled out on the ground, vomiting and in convulsions. Lu jumped up and rushed onto the playing field; his coroner ran close behind.

By the time Lu reached the prostrate figure, he was still. His coroner and another older fellow came up behind and bent over the player.

"He's gone," the coroner said. The older man grimly nodded in agreement.

Lu knelt and touched the young man's hand, then his face. He was remarkably cold. Just moments ago, he was full of vitality and dashing after the ball. Now his body had lost all its warmth, and a thick layer of vomit was smeared over his chin.

Master Wang and Huai-liang broke through the circle of people surrounding Qiu-lin's body. They had heard the coroner. At the sight of his son lying, unmoving, on the ground, Master Wang began to sway and leaned against his oldest son for support.

"Fu Zi poisoning," the coroner declared.

"No. That's not possible," the gaunt older man said. "I'm his doctor. He complained of suffering from yang depletion and wanted a tonic. I gave him the herb to restore his manliness. That's all. He's been under my care for several months. It couldn't be the medicine."

Eyes wide, Master Wang shook his head as if to push the words "Fu Zi poisoning" away. Then, searching his dead son's face, sobs overtook him and he collapsed, sliding to the ground. Huai-liang tried to lift him, but he resisted, remaining near the body. Finally, he raised his head and looked straight at his doctor. "I don't understand. What happened?"

The older brother again struggled to lift his father. "Father, come with me. Come." He looked at Lu, as if pleading for help.

Lu assisted in pulling the patriarch to his feet. "Go with your son. There's nothing you can do."

Devastation written on his face, Wang nodded and left the field, leaning heavily against his oldest son. They sat with his wife and grandson on the sidelines.

Lu ordered men to remove the body. He needed to examine it, for, as with any suspicious death, it was his responsibility as magistrate to personally determine if the cause of death was natural, accidental, or a homicide.

Lu glanced around for the family doctor and spotted him slinking away down the field. He promptly ordered a couple of men to stop the doctor and hold him for questioning.

Lu grabbed a writing brush from the table set on the sidelines for keeping score. Dabbing the brush into black ink, he quickly wrote a note to his court guards, telling them to come to the house and bring all of Fu-hao's court recording materials. It was imperative for the judge to have accurate notes of every stage of the proceedings. These notes would form the heart of his official report to his superiors.

Before questioning anyone, Lu examined the teapot and cup the deceased used during the break. He smelled the liquid left in the pot and, dipping his finger into it, tasted it. It was the same tea he'd been served. He was glad to see there were a few drops of liquid in the cup. He sniffed and discerned a distinctive acrid and slightly sweet aroma. He held the cup out to his coroner, who, after checking it, nodded. "Fu Zi has been added to his tea."

"And it's not in the pot. So, he's probably the only one who drank it," Lu said. "What do you know about Fu Zi?"

"It is an important medicine for people who are out of balance. Their system is too cold and they need more energy. And, of course, men often use it to increase their libido," the coroner said. "But an overdose means certain death. And, as we've seen, it's not pretty. Although death can be quick, the victim suffers dizziness and blurred vision, then severe pain along with vomiting and convulsions."

"He was murdered then?" Fu-hao asked, brush pausing in mid-air.

Lu shook his head. "It's hard to tell at this point. He could have taken too much by mistake. We'll know more after we question the key people involved." With that, he ordered his guard to bring in the family doctor.

"Why did you try to run away?" Lu demanded of the shaking elder.

"I didn't, Your Honor. I was merely, ah, merely going to offer my services to his mother, Madam Du."

"Then you were going in the wrong direction." Lu said coldly. "Tell me about your prescription."

"Wang's younger son has been married for a year and hasn't yet produced an heir. His wife is under the care of a woman specializing in such things. He came to me."

"And you prescribed Fu Zi," Lu said.

"It's often used for such purposes. I have many happy clients. I promise, Master Wang's son did not die because of my treatment." He clasped one hand over the other at chest level and bowed several times, begging, "You must believe me." He cast a glance around the room until he spotted the coroner. "Ask him, he knows."

"We saw him die," Lu thundered. "He was poisoned."

The old doctor seemed to shrink. "Yes," he said in a small voice. "It appears to be from too much Fu Zi, but I don't know how he could have taken so much. I warned him. I even had his mother keep the medicine in her care, so he wouldn't be tempted to take too much. Sometimes men do, impatient to boost their virility. But it's not hard to get it on the streets. Anyone could have put extra in his tea."

Lu had the family doctor stand off to the side, in case he was needed in further testimony.

Next, he requested Madam Du, Master Wang's wife, come before him.

Madam Du was the oldest son's mother and, as Master Wang's first wife, had always been responsible for running the household—even when his second wife was alive. Further, while the younger son was by Wang's second wife, everyone expected Madam Du to share the role of mother to all her husband's children, however difficult such a feat may be.

The diminutive woman with steel gray hair stood erect in her black-on-black silk dress, her face a picture of concern and sorrow. She was impressive in spite of her age, or because of it, Lu thought.

"Madam Du, I'm sorry for your family's loss, but the court has to proceed as quickly as possible for the good of all, not least your son."

She bowed in silence, indicating her understanding.

"Did you at any time go over to the players' tea table?"

"No, Your Honor. I remained with the women. The maids, under the direction of Master Wang's concubine, took care of the men's...," her eyes flashed to the concubine standing on the side of the room next to Huai-liang, "...the players' needs," she amended. Although she referred to her husband in the most formal manner, showing respect for him and the court, Lu thought he detected an underlying reserve.

"Did you know Qui-lin was taking medicine prescribed by the family doctor?"

"Yes."

"Did you know what it was and what it was for?"

"Yes. Master Wang's son wanted to increase his virility; he wanted an heir. He'd already been married a year and his wife wasn't yet pregnant. I told him it was her fault, but he insisted on increasing his yang energy."

"Where did you keep it?"

"In the storage area, where all the medicines are kept."

"Do you know if he took more than prescribed by the family doctor?"

"The doctor had his individual doses wrapped separately. I never gave him more than the proper amount at any one time."

"Who else had access to the medicine storage area?"

"Besides me, Master Wang's concubine. Just the two of us."

"Why did his concubine have such privileges? Isn't that unusual?"

"Perhaps. But I'm getting older, and I am gradually passing responsibilities to the younger generation." Madam Du kept her eyes downcast as she responded clearly and succinctly to each of his questions.

"Wouldn't your oldest son's wife normally take on such tasks?"

"Master Wang preferred his concubine be given that responsibility, not our son's wife."

Lu looked her over. There was nothing in her demeanor or voice indicating a fragile woman who needed to retire from the responsibilities—and power—of running the household.

"Did your son ask to increase his medicine recently? Perhaps to build his strength for today's ball game?"

She paused for a moment to consider the question before responding. "No, he didn't."

"And both you and the concubine have a key?"

She paused again. "No, I have the only key. Whenever someone needs medicine I give it to Master Wang's concubine. She retrieves whatever is requested."

"Did anyone require medicine recently?"

"Well, Xiao Tai-tai had a headache yesterday and wanted a dose. That's all. Except for Qiu-lin, of course."

Lu released her. Staring after her departing figure, he thought about her referring to the younger son as "Master Wang's son," but the oldest son as "our son."

Next, he called in Master Wang's concubine. The tall, striking athlete moved with grace and feminine comportment as she approached him. Lu almost smiled. He wouldn't have guessed this was the same woman who so aggressively swept over the ball field.

"Xiao Tai-tai," he said, addressing her by the family's designation for her. "You were the one to oversee to the tea and snacks given to the players at break. Did you personally give Qiu-lin his tea?"

In spite of herself, her shoulders slumped slightly. "Yes, Your Honor. I gave both of the teams' captains their tea. The maids served the others."

A movement to the side caused the judge to momentarily look up. He saw Huai-liang in mid-step, as if moving toward her.

The audience standing around the room, intently listening to the testimonies, gasped.

"But," she quickly asserted, "it was the same tea for both of them. I didn't—I wouldn't—alter it. Why would I? What would I have to gain? Perhaps if you look into the other team's players' relationships and pasts, you might find a motive."

Lu was impressed by her self-control. The pluck and quick thinking she displayed earlier on the field was evident as she stood before him. She may be young, he mused, but already she possessed considerable poise. No wonder Master Wang was so taken with her. Still, the listeners in the room, all friends and family of the dead man, grumbled stridently. Judge Lu had no doubt they wanted this outsider and newest addition to the family to be the murderer. The alternative was too serious for them to contemplate.

The concubine also seemed to sense the hostility in the room.

"Master Wang won't be very happy if you blame the innocent," she said loudly.

Shocked at the inappropriate outburst, Lu's assessment of her immediately soured. He was no longer impressed by her, but instead angered by her audacity. The room erupted in calls for her arrest.

"Anyone who speaks in the court without my permission will be removed and given a heavy fine," Lu bellowed. A hush instantly replaced the noise. He glared at the young woman and the crowd. He must maintain order as well as respect for the judicial process.

"And do you have anyone in mind?" Lu asked with an edge to his voice.

"You might ask the cripple, Kong," she said. "Ask what happened to his arm. He would have motive."

This accusation led to another outburst. Lu's rap on the table again brought quiet.

He glowered at the concubine. She remained defiant. Nevertheless, he ordered her to stand aside and called in Kong.

A man who had been on Qiu-lin's team stepped forward. Lu hadn't noticed it on the field because the long sleeves on his robe had hidden it, but now it was obvious the man's right arm ended at the elbow. "You heard Xiao Tai-tai's accusation. What do you have to say?"

A mixture of anxiety, fear, and anger crossed his countenance. Finally, he said, "It was an accident. It happened a long time ago. Qiu-lin and I studied for our exams together. His father had gotten a large supply of fireworks to celebrate the New Year. Qiu-lin wanted to set them off. I didn't want to because they are so dangerous. But he talked his father into letting him do it. He could talk his father into anything. When I was holding one of the fireworks, he brought a light too close to it before I could move back. It tore my arm off." He shot a quick glance at the listeners. "It was fate."

"Did you learn how to use a writing brush with your left hand after that?" Lu asked.

"Yes, but not well. I admit that even today my hand-writing looks childish."

Lu knew the significance of a good hand in writing when taking the all-important exams—the provincial and national exams that determined a man's success and place in life. "Did you go on to take the exams?" he asked quietly.

"I tried, but I failed several times at the provincial level."

A sigh of commiseration rose spontaneously from those in the room.

"How do you support your family today?"

Kong looked away. "I haven't married. Who wants a cripple for a son-in-law?" he asked bitterly.

Lu could feel the weight of Qiu-lin's thoughtless actions on the listeners in the room.

"But I didn't hurt him. We're like brothers. That accident, years ago, was my fate. Why would I wait until now to kill him?"

Lu asked a few more questions and then let him step to the side with the others.

Next, he called Huai-liang, the oldest son, before him.

"Huai-liang, where were you during the tea break?"

"I was at the table with all the other players," he said.

"Did you notice anything unusual, anything that could help the court?"

"We were excited about the game. There was a lot of ribbing about which side was going to win and by how much. The usual."

"You brothers were always the captains on opposite teams?"

"Yes. We're competitive and play hard to win. Father likes a good game. He likes to see us pitted against each other. Let the best son and team win."

"Besides Xiao Tai-tai, did you see anyone else near your brother's teacup?"

He shot a quick glance at his father's concubine. Lu couldn't read the emotion on his face. "She filled his cup first, then mine. He drank his in one gulp. The maid Lily refilled it."

"Lily? Who does she normally attend?"

"Mother. She's a new maid with a tendency to get above herself. She has complete access to all of Mother's things."

"Everything?"

"Yes. From Mother's everyday items to her more protected things, like keys to various supply cupboards and rooms."

"You're sure?"

"Quite. Mother runs a tight household, but I've been in her rooms when Lily appears to have too much freedom." Then, as if just thinking of it, he said, "She could easily have gotten a hold of the keys to the medicine cabinet."

"Even so, what would be her motive?" Lu asked.

"Who knows? Maybe my brother asked her to get more Fu Zi for him. I know he desperately wanted to build up his energy, especially for our game today. He knew how much it meant to Father."

Lu excused Huai-liang and mulled over the testimonies he'd heard. Who was telling the truth and who was lying? He needed more information. He called in Master Wang.

"You are now sixty years old. At this stage in life, most men step down and enjoy the fruits of their labor. Were you planning on doing that?" Judge Lu asked.

Wang, who looked like he'd aged ten years in the last couple of hours, nodded. "I was going to divide my property between my sons, one-quarter each, and relax. Enter a new stage of life."

Lu stroked his chin. Such plans were typical. "And what about the other half of your property?"

Wang shrugged. "Of course, I need something to live on.

My younger son would manage it for me until I died and then he would inherit it all. Naturally, he would also continue to care for Madam Du and Xiao Tai-tai, should they survive me."

"Who else knew of your intentions?"

"My sons. And my wife. I told them last week. Such a plan is not unusual."

Yes, this was the normal course of events. As Master Wang told the court his plans, Lu watched the audience. He caught Huai-liang's momentary scowl and his eyes seeming to seek out Xiao Tai-tai.

Even with his younger brother dead, hearing his father publicly express his desire to leave most of his fortune to Qiu-lin visibly disturbed Huai-liang. Lu considered the proposed uneven division of Master Wang's property: one-fourth to Huai-liang, the oldest, and three-fourths to Qiu-lin, the younger. Such a division could cause serious animosity between brothers.

What Lu hadn't expected was Wang's wife's reaction. A look of disgust, brief but definitely there, flashed across her face. As Lu watched her, he suspected she knew more than she'd told the court. He also began to suspect she was manipulating some of the scenes being played out before him. To get at the truth, he had to be careful in how he proceeded. Madam Du was both female and of the older generation, and the law severely limited how a judge could force information from her. The use of torture was generally expected, even mandated, as a part of the court's search for truth. When dealing with women, the disabled, and the elderly, however, such tools were sharply restricted or denied. Xiao Tai-tai was young, but as a female member of a distinguished family of his community, she also had to be treated with special care. Taking a chance, he decided to use guile.

He straightened up even more and called out, "Guards, I

want you to arrest Xiao Tai-tai on charges of murdering her master's son!"

Master Wang turned ashen gray, eyes round as saucers. A satisfied smirk spread across Madam Du's lips. Stricken, Xiao Tai-tai turned toward Huai-liang. He returned a stunned look.

As the guard reached for the concubine, Huai-liang rushed between them. "No. Not her. She's innocent. I put the overdose into Qiu-lin's cup."

Now Madam Du swooned. Master Wang looked back and forth between his son and his concubine, totally confused. Pandemonium broke out among the listeners.

Judge Lu stared hard at the oldest son. "You killed your brother? Were others involved?"

"No. It was only me. Xiao Tai-tai is innocent. She didn't know anything."

"Why are you telling the court this now? Is it to save the life of this woman, your father's concubine?" He paused, "And your lover?"

Huai-liang hung his head, "Yes."

"Louder," Lu ordered.

"Yes! I admit we are lovers, but she had nothing to do with killing my brother."

At this, Master Wang staggered.

Madam Du seemed to spring to life. "No! No!" she cried. "I did it."

Lu flicked a hand at her, as if dismissing her. "You, madam, are his mother and simply want to save him, to protect him."

She drew herself up. Her tiny frame didn't hide her formidable character. "It was all me. My husband was going to give that gadfly Qiu-lin everything. He was no more than Wang's second wife's offspring. As the oldest and son of his first wife, Huai-liang should be his main heir. He worked hard all these years, yet all he and my grandchild were going to inherit was one-fourth of the estate. It wasn't fair. I had to do something."

"And who would suspect the ever-dutiful wife?" Lu asked, watching her intently.

For a moment, only Fu-hao's brush rapidly sweeping across the paper could be heard.

"It was always about him. My husband never considered others in the family. What we did, how we worked, how we suffered. And then he brought in that concubine." She fairly spit out the last words. "That slip of a woman was out to replace me and even deny Huai-liang's wife her place in running the household."

"And then finding out his decision on how to divide the inheritance was too much," Lu said.

"It was absurd. Something had to be done. All that was necessary was for me to put the overdose of Fu Zi into Qiu-lin's tea and have my maid serve it to him. No one knew anything."

"And if anyone did suspect murder, you had set it up so that Xiao Tai-tai, who had access to the medicine room, would appear guilty."

"It was so simple," Madam Du said.

Master Wang looked around the room, aghast. His younger son was dead; his wife of forty years was a murderer; and his concubine was having an affair with his own son. It was all he could do to remain standing before the judge and his community.

Originally published as "The Unseen Opponent, from Judge Lu's Ming Dynasty Case Files" in *Charlaine Harris Presents Malice Domestic 12: Mystery Most Historical*, eds. Verena Rose, Rita Owen, and Shawn Reilly Simmons (Wildside Press, 2017), page 51-62.

CHAPTER 10
THE DEADLIEST POISON

Judge Lu entered the hushed temple at a solemn, dignified pace, leading a line of officials and colleagues. He approached a massive altar draped with the image of a writhing, golden dragon. The Imperial tablet, representing the Ming Dynasty Emperor's presence, sat in the middle of the table. Bronze incense burners, elaborate sprays of fragrant flowers in blue and white porcelain vases, and a pair of imposing bronze candlesticks bordered the tablet. He halted before the altar and stood at attention, as did those behind him.

At the same time, two lines of men entered from the right side of the temple. One consisted of three licentiates—men who had passed the first of three levels of the national examinations—wearing long, blue gowns. Notable local gentry in similar, dark robes comprised the second line. Reaching the altar opposite Judge Lu and his group, the dignitaries halted. The licentiates had the honor of lighting the altar's incense and candles.

Judge Lu watched while the first licentiate proceeded to light the incense sticks to the left of the altar. As the smoke carried the scent of sandalwood throughout the temple, the young man handed the flame to the second licentiate, who lit the incense sticks on the right side. The sandalwood's sweet-woodsy aroma blended with and finally overcame the flowers' lighter scent. Lu breathed in the familiar, heady perfume.

As the second licentiate returned to his position, he handed the flame to the third blue-robed man, who lit the candles. The brightness of the flickering flames bounced off the dragon's silk embroidered stitches. Its fierce eyes glared at the audience, and each golden scale glistened like the night fires in a war encampment.

After kowtowing three times and touching their heads to the ground nine times in front of the Imperial tablet, Judge Lu and the other participants rose. At the sounding of a drum, young students with strong, sonorous voices came forward one at a time to read the Sixteen Maxims in the Sacred Edict, each Maxim a rule for proper behavior set out by the Emperor.

The order and formality of the ceremony pleased Judge Lu. Even before taking on the position as magistrate, he had heard of this troubled and unruly district. Former magistrates had not been able to bring it under control and had suffered the consequences. So now, at this first ceremonial reading of the Sacred Edict under his administration, he was establishing a pattern of teaching his constituents proper values and behavior. By his decree, this educational meeting would be repeated throughout his district. Men in every clan, village, town, and city would be meeting and reading the Sacred Edict at this same time. A sense of satisfaction filled him as he listened to the young voices carrying the message to the town's people assembled in the temple's hall.

At the last Maxim, he stepped forward to address the crowd. "You have heard the Sacred Edict and now understand both what is good and how to prevent evil's survival. Through your good behavior, you increase your reputation and hold high that which is virtuous, thus bringing peace and order to your family, neighborhood, community, and country."

After a few more words encouraging upright behavior, Judge Lu stepped back to once more pay obeisance to the Imperial tablet. Then he and the other officials left the temple proper and went into its courtyard, followed by a line of men carrying the Dragon table within a protective wooden canopy.

The procession of licentiates, gentry, and students came next. As this last group entered the courtyard, Lu narrowed his eyes, pursing his lips in disapproval. The second licentiate moved with sloppy posture, dragging his feet, shoulders down and eyes on the ground. Lu made a mental note to talk to him about proper comportment. Such disrespect before the Imperial tablet set a bad example and could not be tolerated.

"Your Honor."

Judge Lu pulled his attention away from the errant licentiate. At his elbow stood a man wearing an ankle-length robe, its full, draping sleeves badly worn. The robe told Lu much about the man. The style indicated he had significant stature within the community, but had not passed any of the Imperial exams and, therefore, achieved the special rights and privileges they conferred on successful candidates. At the same time, its deteriorated condition suggested its owner was experiencing economic problems.

Seeing he had Lu's attention, the man continued: "Through your guidance, the readings of the Sacred Edict have certainly reached every heart. They are sure to bring order within our community."

The obsequious tone annoyed Lu, but he had come to expect it, especially when the speaker was about to request a favor. He waited for the request that, no doubt, would come.

Suddenly, a cry went up from across the courtyard, "Wait! Move away! Give him room!"

As Lu turned his attention towards the commotion, a student rushed up to him. "Licentiate Xiao has collapsed."

Without pause, Lu cut through the crowd still filling the temple courtyard. He reached the prone figure lying on its right side just as the local doctor knelt to assist. The doctor examined the man's limp left hand and felt for a pulse.

"How is he?" Lu asked, squatting down next to him.

The doctor slowly shook his head. "He's dead." He gently put the deceased's hand down and turned the body over so that it lay on its back before continuing his examination.

Lu studied the youthful face, which was marred by a slick line of drool slipping out of the corner of his mouth. The earthy odor of the courtyard's hard-packed dirt floor encased the body.

This was the licentiate the judge had noticed slouching out of the temple.

"How could a young man die so suddenly?" Lu asked.

"Perhaps the angry gods punished him. With his history of crimes, his participation in today's ceremony must have offended the Emperor and our ancestors."

Lu recognized the high-pitched male voice. A murmur went up in the crowd. Some nodded while others shook their heads. Lu stared up at the blue-robed speaker.

"Ah, Licentiate Wu. Those are harsh words for a man who just passed away," Lu said, rising to address the young man.

Before Wu could respond, however, he was interrupted with: "What nonsense! Licentiate Xiao was an honorable man. Unlike you."

Wu thrust his head toward the speaker, another of the licentiates. "Ji! You're undoubtedly next in line."

Ji started to close the gap between them, fists clenched.

Judge Lu stood, inserting himself between the men.

Scowling, he said, "You two disgrace your official robes when you behave this way. Where's your sense of respect?"

Both men stepped back, hands at their sides, with faces temporarily—and quickly—wiped clear of anger.

Lu turned his attention back to the figure lying on the ground and dropped to his haunches once more. The doctor continued examining the dead man's head and neck. He opened the robe to inspect the chest, then pushed up the sleeves to view the arms, wrists, and hands. After a moment, holding the right hand, he sat back on his heels and stared at Lu.

"I think there's a problem."

"Yes?" Lu said.

"Look at the back of his hand," he said, extending it toward the judge.

An irritated, thin, red scratch ran over it. Hardly a graze and, to Judge Lu, not especially noteworthy.

"And?" Lu said.

"I can't be sure until I know more about how he was acting before he died, but it's possible this scratch tells us about the cause of death."

Lu examined the scratch again. Was he missing something? "Can you be more precise?"

"As far as I know, Licentiate Xiao had no previous health problems. In fact, he was quite robust. While he could have had a hidden illness, there may be a simpler explanation. Poison."

A gasp went up from the crowd and angry buzzing filled the temple's courtyard.

Lu narrowed his eyes, examining the scratch even more closely. It still didn't strike him as a serious injury—serious enough to kill a healthy man.

"You're sure?"

"No, I'm not. However, I've worked in the south for many

years and have seen cases where people died from the deadly venom of snake bites. The symptoms look familiar. I need more information to be sure."

Lu nodded.

He ordered his guards to escort the ceremony's main participants back into the temple proper for questioning.

After everyone had reconvened, they stood silent and morose, avoiding eye contact with each other. Only the incessant murmur of the crowd outside could be heard, an ominous backdrop to their proceedings.

Standing on the raised platform at the front, Lu addressed the assemblage. "I want each of you to think about how Licentiate Xiao appeared today. Did he act unusual in any way? Did he say anything or complain of not feeling well? Think. What do you remember?"

"I talked to him before the ceremony began and he looked and sounded normal," one man said. A couple other young men nodded in agreement.

"How about during the ceremony?"

Licentiate Ji said, "I was standing next to him and handed him the flame; he was fine."

Lu glanced at Licentiate Wu.

"Hmm-hum. Oh, yes." Wu said as if distracted. "No problems."

Lu waited. Finally, the gentry who had cornered Lu earlier said, "Now that I think about it, he did seem to be lagging as we left the temple. I thought I saw him clutching his chest and struggling for breath."

"Yes, I saw that, too," another noted. "I asked him if he was all right. He shook his head. Then he stumbled and I reached for him, but he pushed me away. He resisted offers of help and insisted on walking unaided. He was a proud man."

Lu nodded, thinking of Xiao's slumping as he walked out in the procession. "Doctor, what does this tell you?" he asked.

"It confirms my belief he was poisoned," the doctor said.

"What?" "How could this be?" "Who would do such a thing?" "This doesn't make sense!" The questions and comments fell over each other at the doctor's pronouncement.

"Licentiate Xiao had only one enemy in this room," Ji said loudly and clearly. The others fell silent. "And that is Wu."

The men around him started to protest.

"Are you accusing Licentiate Wu of poisoning Xiao?" Judge Lu asked.

"No. I'm only pointing out what everyone here already knows," Ji said.

Lu studied Ji intently, then looked around the room at the others. A few nodded grimly; the others remained reserved, guarded.

Wu said, "Yes, we had disagreements. That's common knowledge. However, do you think I would be stupid enough to kill him? Everyone would suspect me." He stood firmly while opening his hands in a large, encompassing gesture. He turned slightly toward Ji. "If he died by poison, you have only to look for someone who knows and understands such things. Like *gu* poisoning."

An explosion of excited comments filled the temple.

Ji blanched at the mention of *gu* poisoning. With his face contorted in anger, he said, "What nonsense! It's outrageous for you to suggest such a thing!"

Lu looked from one man to the other. He didn't intervene. Being new to the area, there was a lot he didn't know about the complexities of personal relationships—the friendships and hatreds—between local families. Letting the men rage at each other gave him valuable information he might not be able to get otherwise.

Wu glanced at Lu. "Did you know that Ji's concubine is an outsider—a Miao woman?"

Lu immediately understood Wu's implication. *Gu*, considered one of the deadliest poisons, was widely associated with the ethnic Miao from China's mountainous south. People believed they used the poison as a frighteningly effective means of murder.

Ji started to move towards Wu, but Lu's guard thundered forward, grabbed hold of him, and held him back. The others shrunk away, putting distance between themselves and their colleague.

"I have heard of this *gu*. It's more legend than truth," Lu asserted.

"No indeed," Wu said, sneering at Ji. "The five most poisonous animals are placed together in a container where they kill each other off. The survivor's venom is used to make *gu* poisoning. It's as real as this murderer standing before us."

The crowd's mood turned ominous. They began to form a circle, moving to surround Ji.

"Confine Licentiate Ji in the unused staff room until further notice," Lu commanded his guards.

Ji's skin turned a sickly gray; moaning, he sank against a guard who had come up to take him away.

Lu searched among the faces until he spotted the Education Commissioner. "Sir, before we proceed, I'd like to see you in my chambers. We'll continue with our investigation afterwards."

The commissioner nodded. To punish a licentiate while he still held his position was illegal. It would be an insult to the position itself, to all who held it, and, therefore, to the Emperor himself. Only the Education Commissioner could remove a licentiate status, thereby allowing the magistrate to treat the man as an ordinary citizen under the law. The crowd's murmurings grew with approval. They were certain that if poison killed Xiao, Ji had to be guilty.

Judge Lu sat at his desk, the Educational Commissioner rigid in a chair across from him.

The commissioner cleared his throat. "This is a sad day. I've never had such a duty asked of me before." Clearly, he also believed Lu held Ji because the judge had already determined the young man's guilt.

Lu did not immediately disabuse the elderly man of that notion.

"Wu did not formally accuse Ji," the commissioner went on. "He was only offering comments. The evidence against Ji is weak. Do you think it would hold up upon closer examination by the Superior Court?"

Lu sighed and absently rolled his brush back and forth on its inkstone. All cases were reported to the Superior Court. In serious cases, such as this one, every detail would be carefully reviewed.

At the same time, every loophole would be exploited to its full extent by Ji's clan and their numerous influential supporters. Finding him guilty of the murder would blacken the name of not only his immediate family, but also that of his entire clan. Further, the loss of his status as a licentiate would affect everyone related to him socially and economically. Guilty or not, his supporters would certainly all do their best to protect the young man.

"I have not determined guilt. Nevertheless, I must hold Ji in the protection of the court after Wu's charge before the community," Lu said.

"Yes, the crowd was becoming ugly," the commissioner said. "Who knows what might have happened if you hadn't detained him."

"You have lived here for many years. What do you know of these three men?" Lu asked as he leaned back in his chair.

Spreading his hands over his knees, the commissioner said, "The Wu and Ji clans have been at odds for several generations."

Lu ordered his servant to bring tea. This was going to take a while and he wanted the commissioner to be at ease.

"It all began," the commissioner went on, "when a young woman from the Ji family married into the Wu clan and committed suicide within a few months of the wedding. The Jis demanded compensation, claiming mistreatment forced her to commit suicide. The Wus denied it, of course, and counter-claimed she'd been unstable. They believed they'd been given fraudulent information about the girl and were themselves the victims."

"This tale involves the Wu and Ji families. The deceased, however, is from the Xiao clan," Lu pointed out.

The commissioner nodded. He sat thoughtfully for a short time, straightened his gray robe over his knees, and continued. "Indeed. The Xiao clan is quite small and has managed to do well by aligning themselves with the Jis over the years. In a way, you might consider them to be little brothers to the Jis."

Lu nodded. Everyone needed powerful allies to survive the vicissitudes of life—whether it involved something as simple as altering assessed taxes or as complex as supporting a promising student in the hopes that he would pass the all-important national examinations and thereby gain special legal protection for the whole clan. He made a mental note to find out where the clan and family fault lines fell. Such insight would prove invaluable in guiding his understanding of information. It could both enlighten his decisions and help him avoid disastrous pitfalls.

"This particular Xiao, while quite young, was unusually assertive and had developed a large following. Although he'd only passed the first examination level, his contemporaries regarded him as the most brilliant and promising of their generation. He spoke well and forcefully. He was genial to those he wanted to court and ruthless to those who crossed him." The commissioner paused. "Much like young Wu on all those counts. The two were like twins but on different sides of the road."

"Interesting, but how would that cause one to murder the other? After all, you've indicated their clans have disagreed for many years," Lu said.

The commissioner rubbed his hands over the top of his legs. "True. However, in their case, the competition was excessive."

"What do you mean by *excessive?*" Lu asked.

After another pause, the commissioner said, "You'll find there are two gangs in our district. Much of the criminal activity can be traced to the Jis and Wus and, although the security team knows this, nothing can be done. The gangs are well-protected; they are the foot soldiers, so to speak, of these families." He looked Lu in the eyes. "I'm sorry to say it, but that is the case."

"Why haven't the gangs been disbanded by the military?"

"Relationships and generous gifts."

"Enough said." Lu leaned forward and pressed his fingers together, forming a resting point for his chin.

The two men sat in reflective thought for some time. Lu frowned. While this cast a shadow over the case, he couldn't free Ji. He was quite certain the citizens would take mob action against the young man. For both the murdered man and for Ji, he had to discover who the murderer was. Who had the motivation, opportunity, and means to kill Xiao?

The sound of Lu's servant filling their cups brought him out of his short reverie. He stirred, staring hard at the commissioner.

"Right now, I'll hold Ji. Keeping him here will protect him

from possible mob violence out of fear of his knowledge and use of *gu* poison. At the same time, it will cause the real criminal to relax, believing the case is closed."

"A wise decision," the commissioner said and rose to leave.

The elderly man had only just departed when a servant appeared announcing a local teacher and one of the students who had read from the Maxims earlier. Judge Lu told the servant to bring them in.

"Honorable Sir, my student has something to tell you about today's incident. He is Licentiate Ji's nephew."

Lu inspected the young pupil standing at his teacher's side, eyes politely aimed at the judge's chest. Only the bright red color spread over his face betrayed his terror at appearing before such a powerful official.

"What is it you'd like to tell me?" Lu asked, his voice soft and encouraging.

The boy opened his mouth to speak and emitted a rasping sound. He swallowed and started again, this time with a stronger voice. "Honorable Sir," he said, mimicking his teacher, "before the ceremony started—when we lined up in the courtyard and people crowded around us—I saw a man acting strangely. I noticed him because he seemed to be staring at the licentiates a long time before walking in their direction. As he approached them, he stumbled. Licentiate Xiao reached out to catch him. Before he could take hold of the man, Licentiate Xiao suddenly jerked his hand back. The other fellow seemed to quickly regain his footing and walked on," the boy stopped.

"Did you recognize the fellow?" Lu asked, expecting him to say it was Licentiate Wu.

"Yes...no." He stopped, flustered.

"Take your time," Lu said.

"I don't know his name, although I could recognize him again," the boy said. "He was the fellow talking to you after we all came out into the courtyard. The one wearing an old robe and hat."

Lu was impressed by the boy's sharp observations.

"You're sure?" Lu asked.

"Yes, Your Honor."

"What makes you so sure? There were many people in the courtyard. You could have been mistaken," Lu said.

"I had seen him before, at the Xiao house. He came pleading for help—something about taxes. He didn't want to pay any. Licentiate Xiao wouldn't help."

Lu's demeanor turned stern. "How would you know this?"

The red in the boy's face had receded as he spoke and gained more confidence, but now it rose to his hairline once more. He looked down at the floor. "I sometimes study with his son and I happened to be near a window and heard them talking," he said.

"Hmm," was Lu's only comment. "Do you know why he wouldn't help the fellow out?"

The boy stood silent. His teacher slapped him on the head, "Tell the Honorable Magistrate."

"Master Xiao demanded a very big gift. He said otherwise it wasn't worth his bother. He was busy. The man begged him to reconsider, saying he had nothing now, but if he didn't have to pay taxes he would have money in the future. Licentiate Xiao laughed. Then the man began cursing him, yelling that no man lives forever."

"Did he say anything else?"

The student shook his head. "Just that Licentiate Xiao's life would certainly be short."

"Your Honor, I know the man my student is referring to.

His name is Ho Shan; he is a traditional doctor and small landowner. He lives near the Xin-Yue Pharmacy."

After they left, Judge Lu called his personal guards, Zhang and Ma, into the office. Immediately, the two appeared at the door. They had been waiting, hoping to be sent out on a mission. Men of action, they were easily bored with the court's daily routine.

"I want the two of you to go into the city and find whatever you can about the Ji and Wu clans and their possible tie-ins with local gangs. Also, find out more about this Ho Shan. And, although Ji may have had access to poison through his Miao concubine, what about Wu and Ho Shan? It would be difficult to find and purchase a poison powerful enough to kill a man. See what you can find, if anything, about those two and their access to such a poison."

"Yes, Sir," they replied with enthusiasm.

Lu looked after them as they hurriedly left the room. As his personal guards, he believed he could trust them —unlike anyone else in this quagmire of social connections surrounding him. His guards were outsiders, like him, and owed allegiance only to him. He shuffled the papers on his desk, wishing he could go out into the streets and investigate personally, instead of sending surrogates.

Early the next day, Zhang and Ma presented themselves to the judge. Before asking them any questions, Lu scrutinized his men. They couldn't be more different: Zhang—a sturdy, robust man—fairly bristled waiting for the chance to share their finding; Ma—thin and wiry—stood with feet apart, eyes bright, but otherwise restrained.

Lu folded his hands together and rested his chin on his fingers. "Tell me what you discovered."

Shoulders back, chest high, Zhang began, "We visited several of the cheap wine shops in the city and talked to the locals. People were not shy. They spoke with ease and familiarity about the gangs. There are a few small, unimportant groups of criminals, but all pay homage to one or the other of two larger gangs. One in particular has become a part of the community's everyday life. It's led by the Wus. From what we heard, they have become a government unto themselves in ruling local businesses and farmers."

Lu's blood pressure shot up. A parallel government! How audacious. No wonder he'd heard so much about the unruliness of this district. They were completely out of control.

"Unfortunately for the Wus," Ma said in his measured tone, "the Ji clan, through young Xiao, has become a threat to their influence and control. It seems everyone was waiting for a showdown between the gangs."

"Anything else? Any indication about when and where this showdown was to occur?"

Zhang and Ma shook their heads. Zhang said, "No, but no one was surprised to hear Xiao died yesterday. Some claimed the netherworld was angry and took vengeance on him because he was a hypocrite in participating in the ceremony. From what we heard, that could easily apply to all three of the licentiates." He glanced at Ma, who added, "The word in the wine shops is that the Wu clan is responsible for Xiao's death."

"Did anyone say how?" Lu asked. "Who had access to such poison?

"It doesn't make sense, but instead of the Wu clan, we might look at the Ji clan. Almost everyone we talked to believed Ji has *gu* poison through his concubine and would use it against anyone at any time. They are anxious, terrified of even offending any member of the Ji clan," Zhang said, adding a completely different possibility. "Ji is said to have a temper. They think he just got angry at Xiao and killed him." He shook his head.

Ma added, "Not as much gossip surrounds Wu, but what there is suggests much. Apparently, a pharmacist in town had been searching for a deadly asp venom and finally came into possession of it. People suspect—although, again, they don't really know—that Wu bought the venom from him. It's the perfect poison. The symptoms are difficult to trace unless you know to look for them: difficulty breathing and speaking, blurred vision, muscle weakness, and drooling."

Lu perked up. This closely resembled how Xiao behaved just before he died, and he'd observed the saliva on the dead man's chin himself. "Good work!"

He rubbed his hands together. "What is the name of this pharmacist and where can we find him?"

Zhang's shoulders drooped. Ma took a deep breath and said, "He ran the Xin-Yue Pharmacy. Unfortunately, the fellow died a couple of days ago. He fell off a steep cliff while collecting herbs."

Lu raised his eyebrows. "That sounds more than coincidental. No one you talked to could say who might have bought the poison?" he asked.

"No one knew anything solid," Zhang said. "It could have been Wu or even Ho Shan. Although Ho Shan seemed to be liked and widely respected for his acupuncture cures."

The information his guards returned with made things even more unclear. Lu pressed his lips into a firm line. The road to justice was foggy and it was difficult for him to see the end of this particular path. Impatient with himself, feeling he was missing something, he nevertheless waved for his guards to take seats. From the beginning of their relationship, he allowed a degree of informality with these two, a demonstration of his trust in them.

"Whoever poisoned Xiao, the question remains: how did he do it? We were all there and nothing seemed amiss." Impatiently, he pushed the papers to the side and scowled, studying his desk as if he'd find the answer hidden in its wood grain.

Now that they'd delivered their findings, the two guards relaxed. They hadn't taken the time to eat since yesterday and were hungry. As Lu sat mulling over the case, Ma picked up a dried plum from the fruit plate on the judge's table. Lu looked up from his brooding and absently followed the motion of Ma's hand when he passed the plum to Zhang.

When the big fellow reached out and took the fruit, Ma slapped the table. "That's it! I know who poisoned Xiao and how!"

Lu's eyebrow shot up in a silent question and he nodded for Ma to continue.

"When Xiao handed the flame to Wu at the ceremony, Wu scratched the back of Xiao's hand. That's the scratch on Xiao's hand. Just a bit of poison on the tip of a needle would be enough to kill Xiao." Ma picked up another piece of fruit. "Look at how Zhang took the fruit from my hand." He held his hand out to Zhang with the fruit held in place in the crux of his first two fingers and his thumb. Zhang lightly closed his hand over Ma's as he extracted the fruit.

"When Wu took the flame from Xiao he could scratch the outside of his hand without anyone noticing."

"Why wouldn't Xiao do anything?" Zhang asked, brows drawn together as he contemplated the fruit in his hand.

"He might not have thought much of it. Also, he was standing before the Imperial tablet and in front of a large audience. What could he do without looking like a fool over such a small scratch?"

Lu smiled. "Ah, your analysis may very well have revealed how the murder was accomplished."

At this high praise from their boss, Ma slicked back an invisible strand of hair and Zhang shot his fellow guardsman an appreciative glance.

"Now I know the most likely weapon for delivering the poison. We have three men who may have had access to deadly poisons, two with enough motivation to kill, and one with the means." With that, Lu ordered Zhang to detain Ho Shan.

Confused, Zhang nevertheless immediately rose to obey. As he did, he cast a baffled look at Ma.

Later, in the judge's office, Zhang reported that Ho Shan had been arrested and was being held in jail. While Lu nodded his head in satisfaction, his guards remained perplexed.

"What made you suspect him?" Ma asked.

Tapping his desk, Lu reminded them of the young boy's description of Ho Shan's falling against the Licentiate Xiao and the victim's reaction. "Now that Ho Shan has been arrested, we'll know soon enough.

"Zhang, I want you to remove Ho Shan's clothing and thoroughly examine it. Let me know immediately if you find anything."

Zhang rose quickly and dashed out.

It didn't take long for his guard to return, a grim grin on his face. He had found the murder weapon—a thin, sharp acupuncture needle—nesting in the bottom of Ho Shan's ample sleeve where he had dropped it after scratching Licentiate Xiao's hand. Once the needle was found, Ho Shan confessed fully.

Later, reflecting on the poison's symptoms and effectiveness, Judge Lu shivered at how quickly and easily desperation in an unruly society can turn to murder.

CHAPTER 11
HIDDEN IN PLAIN SIGHT

T he clash and bang of cymbals and drums exploded throughout the temple's open courtyard. A figure with a white patch painted around his nose and up to his blackened eyebrows, stepped out from behind the orchestra. At his appearance, the ear-splitting cymbals and drums quieted.

The man's elaborately decorated, gold-trimmed, long, red robe fell to the top of his ankles, leaving his feet exposed. He grabbed and shook his startlingly bright green, jade-encrusted belt hanging low around his waist. With an exaggerated swagger, he continued forward. The round wings projecting out on the sides of his black gauze cap trembled with every move.

Reaching the center of the stage he looked out at the audience and called in a loud, solemn voice:

"Take the fortunes of the nation as one's right;
Only pay attention to one's own life or death."

At this misquotation, which completely reversed the famous couplet's meaning, the audience broke out in spontaneous laughter. Almost immediately, this was drowned out by the orchestra resuming its enthusiastic and piercing cacophony of sound, marking the end of the play.

Grinning, Fu-hao leaned closer to his distinguished seat-mate's ear, "There's nothing better than a well-educated magistrate, eh, Older Brother?"

Judge Lu laughed at the comment from Fu-hao, who was not only his younger brother but also his court secretary. "Yes, our Magistrate Hu does get everything mixed up a bit, even as he means well." He rose. "Let's hope our court does better than that," he said good humoredly. Ever since he was a boy, when he came to the folk opera with his father, he enjoyed the comedic *choushang* character called Magistrate Hu, who—while portraying an important government official —was also likable, witty, and humorous in his misquotations, exaggerated body language, and never-quite-right official dress.

"Do you want to meet the actors?" Fu-hao asked. "They're new to our area. I understand they'll be leaving tomorrow and will make their way to Hangzhou."

Lu's response was cut short by a cluster of fast approaching men. His guards, Ma and Zhang, promptly stepped in front of the judge, halting the intruders.

"Honorable Sir," the leader huffed as he clasped his hands in greeting and bowed, "I am Jin Yu-an, warden of this area. I have come to inform Your Honor of the death of Merchant Ye as reported to me by his clerk."

"Tell me what happened," Lu said as he motioned for his guards to step aside.

"Clerk Du Zuo-ding went to Merchant Ye's shop this morning as usual, and found the shop closed. He returned several times during the day, but it was always closed. This puzzled him since Merchant Ye opened every day at an early hour without fail and he had not mentioned any change of plans in his routine. Clerk Du returned home, but frequently came by to see if the store had opened. Finally, by late this afternoon, he could no longer contain his alarm. When he arrived this time, he pushed on the rough, wood-slatted windows and finally one gave way. It was unlocked. He climbed through it and into the shop. Merchant Ye lay on the floor, dead. Du immediately came to report to me."

"Have you seen the body?" Lu asked.

"No, Your Honor. I thought I should alert you as soon as possible. I haven't been to the shop or seen the body."

"Good. We will leave immediately." He glanced quickly at Ma. "Return to the court and bring Secretary Lu Fu-hao's writing materials to Merchant Ye's shop."

Ma gave a sharp bow and left straight away. Lu and Fu-hao followed the warden out of the courtyard. Zhang took up his protective position behind the judge.

"Ye's place is just here," the warden said, pointing to a closed, dark shop adjacent to the theater. A window to the right of the door stood ajar. The warden strode to the door and threw it open. "The clerk closed the door to keep the curious out until you had a chance to examine the body," he said.

Lu nodded in approval. It was his duty to examine the body and determine the cause of death, as well as to find any evidence if the death was not by natural causes. The inquisitive and curious could, and did, not only destroy the crime scene, but often freely took whatever was within sight, leaving the scene devastated. Lu left Zhang at the door to keep the persistent away.

Ma, who had followed almost immediately behind them, entered the shop and gave Fu-hao his writing materials. Fu-hao set his inkstone on the merchant's counter top and began to prepare his ink. Judge Lu walked around the body without commenting until his secretary was fully prepared to take notes. Once a good size jet-black puddle of ink filled the depression in his inkstone, Fu-hao laid out the rice paper, took up his brush, and waited.

Lu began reporting his findings.

"Merchant Ye is lying face up on his back. His face, even in death, seems to express surprise, with his mouth agape and eyes unusually wide open. His tunic has a cut in it just above the waist." Lu indicated for Ma to remove the man's gown. Then, taking a small measuring stick from his sleeve, and avoiding the bloodied floor, he knelt beside the corpse. "There is one wound in the man's stomach." He placed the stick alongside the wound and gave Fu-hao the length and width dimensions of the cut. Eyeing the injury, he added: "The wound appears to be quite deep as if made by a long, thin blade." After further inspecting the body, Lu added, "There are no other wounds. The cause of death is due to the one cut. The victim did not die naturally; he was murdered."

Zhang stuck his head in the door, "Sir, there's a fellow here says he's Merchant Ye's clerk."

"Let him enter," Lu said.

A pale, bent figure wearing a worn, gray robe, approached Lu. His face glistened in the evening light. "Sir, I am Du Zuo-ding, clerk to Merchant Ye for ten years."

"You found the body?" Lu asked.

"Yes, sir. As soon as I saw him lying on the floor, I knew he was dead. I immediately went to inform the Warden."

"Go through the store and tell me if anything is missing."

The clerk stepped behind the counter. "The drawer where the more valuable pawned items are kept is open and empty."

"Can you tell the court what was in it?"

Du took a tattered ledger off a low shelf, opened it and ran a trembling finger down a line of items.

"Three sets of silver earrings, a silver handled knife, twelve dark green jade pieces, one brass Buddha pendant."

Lu nodded. "Copy the list of items and who pawned them." While the clerk busily wrote out his list, Lu inspected the room. Except for the body lying in a pool of blood, everything seemed to be in order. "There's no sign of forced entry," he said for Fu-hao's notes. "Apparently, the door was locked from the inside and the murderer simply left through the window, closing it after him."

When the clerk put his brush down, Lu took the list of items and names. After a quick glance at the paper, he stared at the quiet figure before him. Du stood nearby, eyes on the frayed hem of his sleeves as his fingers mechanically rubbed the material.

"The three sets of silver earrings," Lu said, keeping his eyes on Du, "you pawned them?"

The clerk's chest rose and fell as he steadied his breathing. "Yes. My mother is ill and I needed money for her medicine. I had to pawn her earrings."

Lu glanced around the room. The shop was in a good location and, while spartan, the interior's table, desks, and shelves indicated a solid, successful business.

"Your wages weren't enough to care for her?"

Red colored Du's face. With downcast eyes, he replied, "Medicines are expensive and my mother has been ill for some time. I had no other way," he ended in a hollow voice.

Lu couldn't help but pity the man. He had failed his mother by not being able to provide and care for her properly, by having to pawn her precious treasures. Nevertheless, pity or not, theft was often a reason for murder.

Reading down the rest of the page, Lu recognized the name listed next to the knife. It was the actor Cheng who had so ably played Magistrate Hu in the opera earlier today.

"Do you know any of these other people on the list? Do they live around here?" he asked Du.

The clerk shook his head. "Most people who pawn here are travelers. They arrive in the city with its many temptations and then find themselves short of money. Soon, they have to pawn whatever they can to return home."

"Fu-hao, when we get back to the office, check this list against the government records on travelers. "Ma and Zhang, take two men with you and go to the temple grounds where the theater has been set up. Zhang, remain there and search for the missing items on the grounds and in the troupe's quarters. Ma, bring back the actor Cheng for questioning."

The guards bowed and strode from the room.

Back at the yamen, Judge Lu sat in a chair near Fu-hao's desk, facing outward into the room. "Du Zuo-ding come forward to address the court," he ordered.

Ashen faced, the man quickly rounded the desk and dropped to his knees before the judge.

"Tell me all you know about the murder of Merchant Ye and leave nothing out."

"Your Honor, when I came to work this morning, I found the shop closed and the door locked. I thought this was strange since in my ten years as his clerk, the shop has never been closed. Further, Merchant Ye never told me he would be closing for the day."

"Why didn't you alert the Warden at that time?"

"I thought maybe something important had come up and Ye had to attend to it immediately. I went home, but returned three more times during the day. Finally, I was so alarmed that I decided I needed to get into the shop. It was only then that I tried the window and found it unlocked. I threw it open and went in. That's when I found him on the floor. I immediately left to tell the Warden about the accident."

"Accident?"

"I didn't know he had been stabbed. I only saw him on the floor and not moving. I called to him and he didn't answer. I'm not a doctor, so I went to get the Warden."

Lu observed Du's clutched hands. *Probably to stop their trembling*, he thought. "And what about the missing items, including your mother's silver earrings? You had plenty of time to take them before going to the Warden's."

"Sir, Your Honor, I didn't take anything; I didn't touch anything. I went into the shop from the window, saw Merchant Ye on the floor, called to him, and when I heard nothing, I left immediately to alert the Warden. I swear that is all."

"You may step aside for now, but don't leave the room," Lu said.

Du quickly rose and stepped behind his desk once more.

For a while, only the soft noises from the street filled the room as they waited for Ma to return with Cheng. Finally, Ma appeared with the actor, who was still in his Magistrate Hu costume. At Judge Lu's nod, Ma pushed him forward and told him to kneel before the court. Cheng complied with alacrity. On his knees, he clasped his hands together, held them high in front of his chest, and bowed before the judge.

Lu stared down at the actor. He must have been in the midst of changing when Ma arrived to collect him because, although his face had been scrubbed clean of his comedic face paint, he still wore his flamboyant stage robes. Lu noticed that, as with the clerk, the actor's robes showed well-developed wear patterns, and the bright green jade pieces had chips of paint missing. All signs the troupe is not doing well financially, Lu thought.

"Now, tell the court all about your involvement with Merchant Ye and everything you know about his death," Lu ordered.

The man looked up and began in a strong voice, "Honorable Sir, I have nothing to say. I don't know the merchant. I've never met him."

"Don't lie to the court, Cheng," Lu thundered. "The

merchant's clerk is right here and can identify you, plus your name is in the shop records because you pawned a silver knife."

The man's eyes swept over the clerk and back to the judge. "I'm sorry, Your Honor. I remember now. I did come here to pawn my knife. It's not uncommon for me to need to do that as we travel from city to city, so the event slipped my mind. When we first come into a new place, we need money to set the theater up, after the performances, and we're paid, I retrieve my knife. It's that simple."

"And what do you know of the murder?"

"Nothing, Your Honor, and that's the truth. I was preparing for my role. I know nothing of his murder or of the stolen goods. Besides, it would be too difficult for someone like me to dispose of precious jade pieces."

At that moment, Zhang showed up at the door emanating excitement. Instead of entering and standing at attention until called upon, he stood with one foot in front of the other, as if ready to march forward. A cloth bag hung from his right hand.

Lu glared at him. He knew the court rules forbade interrupting during an examination of a potential witness. The guard didn't flinch at Lu's glare, but looked down at the bag and gave it a slight jerk, drawing the judge's attention to it.

"Step forward and present your findings," Lu ordered Zhang, leaving Cheng kneeling on the floor.

Zhang marched up to Lu and presented him with the bag. "I found this with a silver-handled knife in actor Cheng's chest of clothes."

Lu opened the bag and released a knife onto his lap. "This is evidence of your being involved with the crime of murdering Merchant Ye," he said to the figure on the floor before him.

"No. No, Your Honor. That is the knife I pawned, but I retrieved it earlier."

"With no payment for your theater? Where did you get the money to reclaim it?"

The actor's face paled, but he retained a confident voice, "An old patron, a man I'd known for many years, owed me a small sum of money and repaid it. I didn't have to wait for the company to pay me."

"Du, describe the missing jade pieces," Lu ordered.

"Twelve, dark green rectangular pieces about half the size of my small finger," he said. "Each had a small hole drilled into it. They could be worn as a necklace."

"Or decoration on a belt," Lu added glaring at the now trembling actor. "Zhang, remove his belt and bring it to me."

Zhang took the belt and handed it over to the judge. Lu scraped away more paint near a chipped area on one of the belt's lime green decorations. He blew the debris aside, flicked away a few more fragments of paint, and wiped the cleaned surface, revealing a glowing jade stone.

"Actor Cheng, I am arresting you for crimes of burglary and the murder of Merchant Ye. What do you have to say for yourself? Tell the truth now and the court can take that into consideration in determining your punishment; lie to the court and you will receive the full weight of the law."

The actor's shoulders dropped. "I needed more money. We wouldn't be paid for another couple of weeks and I had debts that couldn't wait. So late last night, when I noticed Ye hadn't closed his shop, I took over a few trinkets to see if I could get some cash. When he saw me come in the door, he thought I'd come to retrieve the knife and took it out of his drawer and placed it on the counter. But when he realized that I wanted to pawn a few other things, he looked at them and just laughed. He wouldn't give me anything. Not one copper. He made me so angry that I grabbed the knife and stabbed him with it. I wouldn't have done it if he hadn't made me so angry." He frowned and shook his head.

———

Later in the judge's chambers, Fu-hao, Ma, and Zhang relaxed with a cup of tea.

"How did you know it was Cheng?" Ma asked. "The knife alone wouldn't have convicted him. It's possible he could have reclaimed it earlier."

Lu looked over at his guard. He was happy to see that Ma was trying to work things out. Ma and Zhang were his personal guards, but also assisted him in investigations.

"Yes. The knife indicated a connection, but would not be proof by itself. However, when Cheng gave his testimony, he mentioned the jade pieces that were stolen. No one outside of the few of us knew what exactly had been taken from the shop. Only the murderer would know that. When he mentioned the jade, I looked again at the belt he wore with his costume. The paint had already started to chip off, revealing a bit of smooth stone underneath. It was a reasonable guess on my part that he was hiding the jade pieces as a cheap part of his costume."

"Ah, hiding in plain sight!" Fu-hao exclaimed.

"It might have worked if he hadn't been over-confident and too talkative." Lu said. "In the end, he gave himself away."

CHAPTER 12
THE SLEEPING SWAN

A persistent cloud cover muted the sun's rays throughout the long day of riding, shielding Judge Lu and his companions from the searing summer heat. The four travelers progressed at a steady pace as they ventured south, tracing the edges of fields, passing over hills of dense bamboo, and traversing a narrow passage between sharply rising karst formations. They rode parallel to the Gan River in their southerly journey.

As they entered a market town hugging tightly to the mountains precipitously rising along its side, an immense, dark shadow slowly reached out to engulf the narrow valley.

Lu sought out the town's low-cost, simple guesthouse, one where even the most frugal traveler might stay. When they arrived, however, it was full.

Astride his horse, Lu sat watching for his guard, Zhang, to return from the town's only other inn. His horse moved restlessly under him. It was tired and knew water and food were waiting. Lu absently leaned forward and patted its neck.

He glanced over at his companions. Ma, his second guard,

sat stoically, waiting. However, Fu-hao, his brother and court clerk, stirred impatiently on his saddle.

"I hope there's room here," Fu-hao mumbled. He waved a hand in the direction of the inn's massive double door. A lantern swung over it, gently illuminating the inn's name: The Sleeping Swan. "At least this place appears more comfortable than that last one. I don't know why you even bothered trying to get a room there." He scrunched his nose in distaste. "Who knows what conditions we'd have ended up with."

"Must I remind you that we're not here for a vacation? With the rise in illegal activity in the area, we must find out who is behind it," Lu reprimanded. "It's the lower-end inns where we are most likely to learn about potential troublemakers. Perhaps even meet them. Not in an expensive inn, such as this."

Fu-hao sniffed. "I don't understand why you insisted on doing this yourself. Why didn't you send out a couple of the court's men to check on it?"

Before Lu could answer, Zhang strode out of the building. "We can stay here. They only have one other guest."

"At last," Fu-hao mumbled.

Lu forbore giving his brother another lecture. Besides, he was ready to rest for the night, too. He slipped off his horse, tossing the reins to Ma, and signaled for his brother to follow him.

They entered a worn but well-appointed room. Clearly, this once impressive inn, had fallen on hard times. A middle-aged man, wearing a soft skull-cap and a mid-length gray coat tied under his ample stomach, approached.

"Welcome, Sir. I'm Innkeeper Huang and I understand you need a room for the night. You arrived just in time, before the coming rain."

His Mandarin was highly accented, but understandable.

Lu guessed the innkeeper to be a local and, therefore, a native Gan speaker who learned Mandarin as a second language. Lu expected most innkeepers to be able to communicate in Mandarin, whatever their own local language.

"You may have your man take your horses to our stable. Will you be wanting supper?"

"Yes. We've had a long day." Lu did not want the innkeeper to know he was the provincial magistrate and, therefore, let the man assume he was a gentleman passing through with friends.

"It will be ready right away. You can eat before you go upstairs to your rooms. My wife, Mistress Yang, prepared an ample dinner." His eyes flicked toward the dining room and at a sturdy, middle-aged matron standing at a round table where a family sat eating.

She was talking and laughing with a young woman who wore a long tunic over a dress with full, flowing sleeves. Every now and then, the younger woman would turn to the tall, dark man sitting next to her, murmur something and, using her chopsticks, place a morsel of food in his dish.

The man's distinctive features and unusual dress caught Lu's attention. He had a broad face and pale, round eyes, and wore a small, embroidered, rimless hat as well as a long, dark coat with gold embroidered design flowing down its lapel. A maid and a wet nurse holding an infant sat nearby.

Lu, Fu-hao, and his guards took another table.

Soon, the stranger's wife and servants left him alone at his table, drinking tea. Lu took this opportunity to lean over and greet him.

In exchanging greetings, Lu learned the man was a merchant called A-zu.

"Have you been traveling long?" A-zu asked.

"We started out in Ji-an early this morning. It was a quiet journey but tiring. What about you?"

"My people are Uyghur from the far west, so we have been on the road for many weeks. My family was relieved to finally arrive here."

"Ah. So, you are planning on staying here a while?"

"You could say so. I intend to build a magnificent guesthouse. The very best. This town sits on a busy north-south route. Merchants and officials must stop on their journeys—whether they travel by river or by land. I aim to serve those wanting both comfort and refinement."

"Doesn't this inn offer that?" Fu-hao asked.

"Mine will be better," he said with a shadow of a smile.

The innkeeper shot the Uyghur an angry look as he placed dishes laden with fish, braised pork, spicy vegetables, and kelp roles on the table.

A-zu noticed and laughed. "Don't worry. Your inn is well-known and will always be profitable."

Lu looked from the innkeeper's stoic face to the dining room. There were no other customers.

Fu-hao lost no time in starting in on the fish. He grabbed a slice of chili and placed it on the delicate fish. Slurping it down, he smacked his lips. "Excellent. You wouldn't find better in Nanchang City itself." He smiled at the innkeeper as he placed the last dish on their table.

At this praise, Huang seemed to relax. He bowed in response and returned to the kitchen.

Lu continued chatting with A-zu until they'd finished their meal. Finally, Lu and his comrades rose to retire for the night.

A-zu remained at the table with his tea. The last Lu saw of him, he was pulling a book out of a satchel and showed no signs of leaving his own table any time soon.

It seemed that Lu had barely closed his eyes when he was awakened by a crash and a scream of pain. He threw on his robe and dashed out into the hallway where he met Zhang and Ma. Leading his guards, they passed the Uyghur's rooms. His wife stood at the door, eyes wide with concern. She took a step forward.

Lu raised a hand to stop her and pointed back into her rooms, indicating she shouldn't come out.

She nodded and retreated while leaving the door ajar.

As Lu clambered down the stairs, the innkeeper ran out of the kitchen and into the dining room, his wife and son close behind.

"A man just ran out the front door!" Huang yelled. Zhang, Ma, and the innkeeper's son dashed out into the street. The light from the hanging lantern dimly lit a patch in front of the inn; the rest was blackness as the heavy cloud-cover hid the night sky.

The Uyghur lay on the floor, a long rip through the back of his robe, blood soaking through his clothing, and an upturned table and broken pottery strewn at his feet. Lu quickly moved over to the body and knelt down to examine it.

"Get away from him," Huang ordered. "I'm head of our town's security team. I'll take care of this."

Waving the innkeeper away, Lu said, "And I am Lu Wen-xue, magistrate of this province."

"How do I know you are who you say you are?" Huang challenged. "Why didn't you register as the magistrate when you signed in?"

"This is, indeed, Magistrate Lu," Fu-hao said as he came down the stairs. "We are on another mission and happened to stop here."

The innkeeper was about to say more when he glanced over at his wife, standing nearby with her hand over her mouth, staring at Lu. He paused, then said: "I am willing to assist in any way necessary, Your Honor."

With the help of his brother, Lu proceeded to examine the man and his wound. He studied the table from where he squatted, then rose and stepped over to the victim's feet.

"It looks like he realized he was in danger and tossed the table to give himself a chance against his assailant. However," Lu retraced his steps and studied the victim, "it appears that while he faced his enemy on the other side of the table, someone struck him from behind."

"His bad fate to die such a death," Huang said.

"Did you see anyone in the room with A-zu after we left?" Lu asked.

"No. After replenishing his tea, I left him to his reading."

"Where did you go?"

"To the kitchen, to make sure things were ready for tomorrow."

"Were you there when you heard the scream?"

"No. I had already retired with my wife and son to our private rooms adjoining the kitchen."

Just then, Zhang, Ma and the innkeeper's son returned. Zhang had a young man in tow.

"I found this fellow in the stables," Zhang said, pushing the captive forward and into a kneeling position on the floor.

"Were there signs of anyone else?" Lu asked.

"No. While Zhang searched the immediate area, we..." Ma waved a hand to include the innkeeper's son, "split up to search the town for the thug. But with the cloud cover, it was too dark."

"There's only the narrow road that runs through the town and a footpath behind these buildings that back up to the mountain," the innkeeper's son added.

Lu turned toward the man kneeling before him. "What is your name and what were you doing in the stables?"

"I am Bari Samadi, Master A-zu's servant. I take care of his horses and sleep in the stables."

Lu looked over at Huang. "Do you recognize this fellow?"

"Yes. It is as he says."

"Tell me what you saw and heard tonight," Lu ordered.

"I was asleep until your men woke me and brought me here."

Lu's eyes narrowed as he studied the young man. He turned toward Zhang. "Can you confirm his testimony?"

Zhang nodded. "He was in his bed when I went into the stables. Asleep or pretending to be asleep."

Lu frowned. There wasn't anything more he could do tonight.

"What should we do about...about...," Huang spoke up, his eyes flickering toward the corpse.

Lu sighed. Since A-zu had died a violent death, his ghost would be angry and could cause trouble to the living. He had to be removed.

"Zhang, Ma, take care of the body. We may as well retire and proceed in the morning."

———

Lu sat up in bed, awakened by the sound of horses snorting. He jumped up and slipped on his robe. Fu-hao, grabbing at his own robe, joined Lu.

"Tell Zhang and Ma to meet me at the stables," Lu said as he dashed out the door.

Lu ran out into the weakly lit night, heading for a barely visible, looming structure. He paused at the entrance, listening and letting his eyes adjust. The horses had settled down. There was no other sound.

Zhang and Ma ran up to him. "Fu-hao is bringing a light," Ma whispered.

Lu pulled the heavy door open. It silently and easily gave way.

"Show yourself. Come out!" Lu called.

Silence.

Fu-hao arrived bearing a lantern, the innkeeper and his son close behind. Lu took the light and indicated that the others should follow him. They all cautiously slid inside.

The air, suffused with the warmth of the horses' bedding and an unexpected sweet, metallic smell, assailed Lu. He held the lantern high in order to cast the broadest light.

The horses whinnied and moved restlessly in their stalls.

Lu pointed to his left and right, telling Zhang and Ma to search those areas of the stable. As they moved away from him, he stepped down the aisle running between the horses.

A bulky shape along the back wall caught his attention. As he approached, he could discern the body of a man covered by a light blanket. He bent down over him and examined his face.

Bari Samadi.

Blood soaked through the covering and into the tamped earth. Lu checked for signs of life. There were none. He examined the wound. It was long and narrow, like A-zu's.

"The poor man," Huang murmured.

"What evil spirits have those foreigners brought upon themselves?" His son spat on the ground.

Lu glared at him. "Such deaths do not come from spirits. We can only look to men for such deeds."

He stood and surveyed the area. Nothing appeared to be out of the ordinary; no obvious signs of disturbance or struggle.

His men came up, reporting they hadn't seen anything unusual.

"It's as if the murderer knew the surroundings well,

allowing him to enter, approach A-zu's sleeping servant, and kill him. But why?" Lu shook his head.

"Perhaps the murderer thought Samadi could identify him?" Fu-hao suggested.

"We won't know until we get more information," Lu said.

"Should we scout the area?" Ma asked.

"No." Lu shook his head. "It's still too dark and he's had plenty of time to get away." He exhaled a puff of air. "We'll investigate more tomorrow."

Once more, Lu lay stretched out on his bed, eyes open. The night's two unexplained deaths kept sleep at bay. There seemed to be no obvious motivation for the killings. Worse, the victims were strangers to the area. There were not many people he could interrogate in order to discover the who and why behind the murders. He sighed. The first thing he needed to do in the morning was to interview A-zu's wife, Madam Ping. She might be able to add something to this puzzling case.

He continued to toss and turn as sleep eluded him. He finally started to doze when the night air filled with yelling and loud noises.

"Honorable Sir, Honorable Sir," came a frantic voice accompanied by a rapid beating on his door.

He swung the door open to reveal the tearful wet nurse. She frantically indicated for him to follow her. She spun around and hurried down the hall.

Lu sprinted after her.

Ma was running down the stairs. "I'll catch him outside," he yelled back at Lu.

As Lu entered Madam Ping's room, Zhang's form disappeared out the window and into the heavy mist. Ping stood in the center of the room, tightly holding onto her baby and crying.

"What's going on?" Lu demanded.

"A man tried to kill my baby," Ping sobbed. "First my husband and now my baby."

"Tell me what happened."

"My wet nurse woke to find a man holding a cleaver over him. She jumped up, screamed, and knocked into him. He dropped his knife and fled out the window," Ping said, trembling as she told her story. "He escaped toward the footpath at the back of the building. Your guard burst into the room as the man was escaping, and went after him."

"Can you identify the intruder?" Lu asked the wet nurse as he bent to pick up the cleaver lying on the floor.

She looked at him and then at her mistress.

"She only speaks Gan, not Mandarin," Ping said in accented Mandarin.

Lu studied the girl. He had assumed that since A-zu was Uyghur the two women were too. However, if the wet nurse spoke Gan, she was likely from Jiangxi province.

As if reacting to his puzzlement, Ping explained, "My wet nurse and I are both from here. My father was a widower and small merchant. He arranged my marriage to Master A-zu to tie the two families together and to ensure that I would be taken care of."

Of course, Lu thought. *That's why Mistress Yang had treated the young woman so familiarly earlier in the evening.*

The thumping of feet rapidly ascending the stairs caused Lu to squint into the hallway. Huang soon materialized at the door.

"I heard yelling and saw Ma running out the front," he said.

Almost simultaneously, his son appeared. "Did she see the

163

thief?" he asked, passing a sleeve over his moist face and working to catch his breath.

"What can we do?" Huang asked.

Lu pressed his lips into a tight line. Without answering the questions, he said, "I'm afraid the culprit escaped into the night once more. Ma and Zhang are out looking for him, but I have little hope." He watched Madam Ping. Even as she held her baby, she trembled.

"Ask your wife, Mistress Yang, to come and stay with Madam Ping. The attack on her son has been most unsettling."

"Yes, Your Honor. Right away," Huang said and hurried out.

Lu turned the cleaver over and over, judging its weight and noting its size. The blade fit the length and width of the wounds on A-zu and Bari Samadi. As he turned it over once more, he noticed that the innkeeper's son seemed to be anxiously watching its movement.

"Do you recognize the cleaver?" Lu suddenly asked him.

The lad started. "No. Yes. That is, it's common enough. Probably every household owns one like it. It's used to prepare fish, onions, meat, vegetables, everything." He rubbed his hand over the side of his head. "And, it makes a powerful weapon."

Lu nodded. Every household would have a cleaver, Lu thought, as he turned it over in his hands. The wooden handle on this one had a worn set of characters on it. So worn that he couldn't read it in the room's weak light.

Huang returned with his wife, who carried a tray of tea with cups. After serving Lu, she poured one for Ping and stood behind the young mother.

Lu placed the cleaver on a table and took up his teacup.

Yang's eyes fell on the cleaver and she shivered.

After asking Huang to translate for him, Lu asked: "Have

you seen this cleaver before, Mistress Yang?"

Yang's hand nervously covered her mouth and she shook her head.

"Come. Take a good look," Lu encouraged in a kindly voice. He lifted it and turned it around in his hand. "Do you recognize this marking?" he continued, holding the handle out to her.

She peeked over at her husband and down at the weapon. After a pause, with her eyes respectfully held low, she replied while Huang translated. "She can't read and doesn't know what the characters mean."

At that, Ping came forward, still clutching her baby. "You mistranslated her words," she said in Mandarin.

With a bland expression, Huang said something in Gan to her.

Ping shook her head. "The Honorable Lu asked if she recognized the mark, not if she could read it, and she did recognize it, worn as it is."

"And what did she say it was?" Lu asked Ping.

"The name of this inn, The Sleeping Swan."

Lu glared at Huang, who immediately fell into an obsequious set of bows.

"Your Honor, while it does have our inn's name on the handle, I didn't want you to draw the wrong conclusion, so I didn't tell you everything at first." Huang looked up at Lu. "Someone stole that very cleaver a week ago."

"Stolen," Lu said without expression. "What else were you missing?"

Huang shrugged his shoulders. "Nothing that I could determine."

"And who do you think came into your kitchen and took this one cleaver?"

"We get many guests, as you know. I couldn't say or I would have gotten it back."

"Is that true?" Lu asked the innkeeper's wife.

In a muted voice, Ping translated this conversation to Yang. "She doesn't know," Ping said.

"Come now, Mistress Yang. You are the cook. How can you not know if your cleaver is missing?"

With her gaze on the baby, Yang finally answered, with Ping translating. "She used that very cleaver yesterday to prepare the dishes for the night's meal. Afterwards, she washed and put it away. That's the last time she saw it," Ping said.

"Lying in an investigation is a criminal offense, Huang," Lu said to the innkeeper, his voice hard-edged.

Before he could continue, however, Zhang stepped into the room, frustration written over his face. "This turtle's egg is either very lucky or a demon," he said, swearing.

"Did you find anything of note?" Lu asked.

Zhang scowled. "I ran along the building to where the path crosses behind the inn, but couldn't see anyone in either direction. He probably slipped into one of the buildings. He wasn't on the path."

"Did you check the buildings for unlocked or open doors?"

"The only unlocked door was the inn's, which opened onto the footpath."

"Huang's?" Lu said.

Zhang nodded.

Just then, Ma strode into the room, caught Lu's eye, and shook his head to indicate he hadn't found anyone.

Lu refocused on the innkeeper's son. "Step forward," he commanded.

The young man stumbled closer to Lu, head down.

Yang cried out and started to rush to her son. Zhang held her back. She stared at her husband, and, in a high-pitched voice, spewed forth a torrent of words.

Angerly, Huang cut his hand through the air as if to stop her.

Yang inhaled deeply and halted. Shoulders slumped, she stood in silence, tears streaming down her cheeks.

"Translate," Lu said to Ping.

"Mistress Yang begged Huang to speak up and save their son, to tell you what really happened."

"And what happened?" Lu asked.

"Something about the need to protect the town from outsiders, foreigners," Ping said, shaking her head.

"Our Most Esteemed Emperor Hongwu overturned the foreign leaders of the Yuan Dynasty, yet outsiders persist in trying to enter and take over from the inside." Huang spat out.

"Father, don't," his son said, stricken.

Huang emphatically shook his fist. "That Uyghur merchant took Ping, a daughter of our village. And ... and then he has the audacity to come back and start a business here. Here. You heard him yourself. He wanted to establish a business which would destroy a long-standing, generations-old inn, The Sleeping Swan. He had to be stopped. He would drive us into poverty."

"And what did you do?" Lu asked. His tone even, without judgment.

"What had to be done. At first, I tried to talk him out of setting up here, but he wouldn't listen. He laughed." Huang smacked his right fist into his left hand. "It wasn't a joke. When I threatened him, he tossed the table and reached toward his shirt. My son thought he was going for a knife and struck him from behind."

His son sagged as if under a weight.

Huang's eyes petitioned Lu for understanding. "He struck that worthless interloper to save me."

"We didn't find a knife on him," Lu said.

"We didn't know," Huang replied, his voice had lost its strength.

"What about A-zu's man? Did you kill him, too?"

Huang and his son remained silent.

"Apparently, he was asleep when killed," Lu said and waited.

After a pause, Huang said, "Just another turtle's egg. He could cause trouble."

Ping pulled her son's head to her shoulder as if to protect him.

"And what about the child? Did you think he was going to cause trouble, too?" Lu asked, sarcasm coloring his tone.

Huang glowered at Ping holding her son. "You are better off without him. With no half-breed son, you could remarry."

Ping turned away from Huang.

"It was you who attempted to kill the baby tonight?" Lu said, swiveling toward the young man, remembering how he had wiped his face when he'd first entered the room. Lu now also observed his damp clothing.

The youth nodded.

"Speak up," Lu commanded.

"Yes," he muttered.

"Zhang, Ma, take these two into custody. We'll go to the yamen tomorrow where they will stand trial," Lu said.

The next morning, before Lu left for the yamen, Ping approached to say good-bye and thank him for giving her husband and servant justice.

"What will you do now, Madam?" Lu asked. "Will you remain here?"

She shook her head, her lips pressed tightly as she looked at their surroundings. "I will return to my husband's home-town and raise our son there, among his father's people. His people."

ACKNOWLDEGEMENTS

As has been famously pointed out many, many times, no book is a product of one person. We authors all have others who support us and our art in many ways. I have been privileged to have the support of my wonderful editor, Renee De Voe Mertz, who patiently goes through all of my work; of my sharp-eyed spouse, Ronald Mertz, who willingly reads and, yes, even listens to my work; and to Kelly Cochran, who has an unfailing eye for the visual in helping me with my covers. For this particular volume, I also had three wonderful beta readers, who in every way have made this a better book: Susan Zahra, Jennifer L. Jacoby, and Sue Atwell. Thank you all!

NOTE

I hope you enjoyed reading **Judge Lu's Case Files, a collection of short stories**. If you did, please consider leaving a review on the site where you bought the book. Your comments will help other readers find their way into the life and times of Imperial China.

Also, for more mysteries that bring late 14th century China to life, go to padevoe.com.

Best in all your mysterious reading adventures!

OTHER MING DYNASTY MYSTERIES & ADVENTURES BY P.A. DE VOE

Lotus Shoes, a short story from ancient China

Hidden, A Mei-hua Adventure

Warned, A Mei-hua Adventure

Trapped, A Mei-hua Adventure

Mei-hua Trilogy, a box set

Deadly Relations, A Ming Dynasty Mystery

No Way to Die, A Ming Dynasty Mystery

To discover more stories about Imperial China,

visit: padevoe.com